HIS CHRISTMAS LOVE

A Cuffs & Spurs Holiday Novella

ANYA SUMMERS

Published by Blushing Books
An Imprint of
ABCD Graphics and Design, Inc.
A Virginia Corporation
977 Seminole Trail #233
Charlottesville, VA 22901

Anya Summers
His Christmas Love

EBook ISBN: 978-1-947132-67-2
Print ISBN: 978-1-947132-68-9
v1

Contents

His Christmas Love

A CUFFS & SPURS HOLIDAY NOVELLA

Author's Note

Dearest Reader,

Thank you so much for purchasing His Christmas Love! This sexy, short novella, while set in the world of Cuffs & Spurs, introduces a whole new set of characters we've not met previously. There will be plenty more Cuffs & Spurs stories to follow. Enjoy Hannah's naughty Christmas adventure!

Happy Reading!

~ Anya Summers

Chapter 1

What a Christmas!

There was nothing quite like having your live-in boyfriend forget the holiday.

Hannah had been dating Brady for two years. Two incredible years filled with laughter, love and kinky times at the local lifestyle club, Cuffs & Spurs. They lived together. She'd moved into his house with him last January. Brady had made room for her here, in what was now their home. He'd never begrudged her space or the decorating of it, just told her how empty his life had been before she became a part of it.

Hannah loved Brady, adored the sexy man with all her heart and soul. Brady was it for her in the romance department. When she thought about her future, what she saw was him, at her side as her partner in crime. And yet, this morning there'd been no 'Merry Christmas,' or 'the house is decorated beautifully, babe.'

Nothing. Nada. Zip.

And it made her feel like a horrible, insipid shrew that she wanted the words, that she *needed* the words. That the reassurance, the praise, somehow affirmed that she was worthy of his love.

They were her issues. She knew that. And she had been working on them, and the lifetime of neglect. As someone who'd been raised in foster care and spat out on her own at eighteen, she had grown up feeling unwanted and unloved. It was why she taught second grade at the local public school and watched out for each of the kids as if they were her own—because she, more than anyone, knew how it felt not to have anyone care—short of the government check you brought in.

But thanks to her background, Hannah ended up clinging to acknowledgements of praise as some sort of litmus test that she had to pass. It was what made Brady different from any of the men she had dated. The sexy firefighter was warm and giving. When he was home, he was constantly touching her; even if they were just watching a movie together, he would put his arm around her and cuddle her close.

He had soothed her ravaged soul, but it was at times like these that her old issues of abandonment and neglect tended to rear their ugly heads. Not to mention, the holidays were hard when you didn't have a family. She wasn't close to her foster parents and their kids. Never had been, and never would be.

And maybe it made her cling too tightly to Brady, because he was the best thing in her life.

Hannah sighed. She should just call it a day and get over herself already.

It was just that this was their first Christmas living together as a couple. And she had worked to make this holiday special, to show Brady how it could be for them, not just this Christmas but for what she hoped were all their Christmases together. It stemmed from her abandonment issues—the unrelenting urge to be loved, and have someone want to keep her, not as a burden but because they wanted her.

Hannah had decorated the interior of their ranch style home in the suburbs of Jackson Hole with unrepentant, tasteful glee. Over the last month, she had baked huge batches of Christmas cookies for Brady to take to work. She had wrapped presents, hung the stockings and decorated the tree. She had risen shortly after he'd left this morning and slaved away in the kitchen, cooking up the perfect holiday feast.

But he'd not made it back in time for Christmas dinner.

Nor had he called to tell her he wouldn't make it home for dinner. Granted, if he was in the middle of a call, he couldn't. She got that, understood how important his job was, but it was bringing up all her old wounds.

She'd picked at the dinner she'd spent the day cooking and packed it all up: the turkey, the stuffing, the mashed potatoes, the green bean casserole, the roasted carrots, and candied yams. The pies were covered up and stored away in the fridge with everything else. Then, to top it off, Hannah felt silly dressed in a naughty Missus Claus costume. She had wanted to surprise Brady with it, watch his gaze go dark with lust as she served him dinner.

Instead of having a Christmas quickie in the kitchen, here she was in the living room, an empty glass of wine in her hand, reclining on the sofa by the fireplace. Alone. On Christmas.

Hannah sighed at the sight of the unopened presents beneath the lit tree.

It wasn't Brady's fault. She knew he'd been exhausted when he'd left for work before the sun had risen this morning. Off being a hero, saving lives as a firefighter with the Jackson Hole Fire Department, he was part of engine crew 3127. She couldn't be prouder of him. He and his crew had battled a house fire last night.

At least it was a house fire and not a forest fire. Brady had worked as a hot shot and told her hair-raising stories. Hannah knew without a doubt that he was likely risking life and limb once more, while she pouted.

And it made her feel like the most horrible person in the world. Like she shouldn't be feeling neglected on Christmas, when other people in the world were losing their homes and everything they had worked for all their lives.

Tired of feeling sorry for herself, she rose from her seat on the burnt cinnamon leather Chesterfield sofa by the tree and fireplace. The fire she'd lit early today was now little more than red glowing embers. So much for having a holly, jolly Christmas. She closed the glass doors. The fire would peter out soon enough.

Hannah ambled into the kitchen with her empty wine glass, dejected and more than a little hurt. She poured herself another glass of wine, thinking that perhaps a relaxing bubble bath was in order, and she was about to toast the idea, when big, warm hands slid around her waist and pulled her back against a delicious hard male body.

"You're home," she sighed. Brady. God, she loved him, and was amazed that a simple touch could still take her breath away. Hannah knew that Brady loved her—even if he'd forgotten Christmas, at the end of the day, that wasn't important. But as she melted in the embrace, her internal sensors registered different pheromone levels and that his scent was all wrong. Brady smelled like cedar forest and rugged male, whereas whoever's arms were around her carried a hint of amber with some deeper, darker notes and an undercurrent of testosterone.

She stiffened. Alarm bells dinged internally.

Then Brady appeared in front of her, stepping into her line of sight. He was, without a doubt, a walking wet dream. His six-foot, rock-solid form was dressed in nothing but a pair of well-worn blue jeans, slung dangerously low around his lean waist, displaying the top portion of the victory lines she loved so much and his firm, broad chest dusted with a smattering of hair that was a smidge darker than his sun-streaked dirty blond hair. The man never failed to make her blood simmer with just a simple glance. Testosterone oozed off him. But the thing was, if Brady was standing in front of her, whose arms were wrapped around her?

"Brady, what's going on?" she asked with a hint of unease lacing her voice as she stiffened against the hands holding her.

"I thought I'd give you your Christmas present. You remember Gavin, babe?" Brady said with a chin nod toward the man behind her.

At his name, Gavin's mouth descended on Hannah's neck and nibbled on that one spot at the base where it met with her shoulder, which turned her into a heated puddle of arousal at the feel of soft lips and whisker stubble. Her nipples hardened and she squeezed her thighs together at the sudden pulsing from her sex.

"Yes," she said, her voice a breathy whisper. Her hands clenched around the wine glass. She remembered Gavin; more than she should. He was wickedly sexy, soulful, and Brady's best friend. But why was Gavin touching her, kissing her neck and making her yearn for more? The heat from his solid form surrounded her and she was melting against him. What was happening?

"Well, tonight, I wanted to give you the fantasy. *Your* fantasy... of being with two men, as part of your Christmas present. And I love your costume. Have I told you how fucking gorgeous you are?" His dark gaze was a caress as he sauntered closer, his swagger confident. Like a big jungle cat that knew he was at the top of the food chain and had just spied his meal.

Everything inside her felt electrified. Two men? They had chatted about their fantasies, sometimes used those fantasies as dirty talk while they were in bed. Brady loved when she role-played and dressed in skimpy costumes. She adored it when he went all caveman and dominant on her, tying her to the bed and pulling out the flogger. When she'd mentioned wanting a three-some with two men, she'd never thought it could become reality. It was just dirty talk while he broke out the cock ring with the dildo attachment. She had even pestered him about why he didn't have the typical male fantasy of being with two women.

His answer was always that she was more than enough woman for him. He really was that deep in the soul, yummy goodness.

It was a dream; a naughty, kinky, pleasure-filled dream of hers to be taken by two men at once. Her earlier malaise was forgotten. Of course Brady would never forget her on the holidays. It had all been in her head, with echoes of her past resurfacing. But she protested—albeit feebly.

"But I love you, Brady. I don't know that this," she bit her bottom lip as Gavin's large hands cupped her breasts and began kneading them through the fabric of her tiny red dress while nipping at her earlobe, "um, is a good idea."

Especially when her body was ordering her to be quiet.

Brady was close enough that she could feel the heat pumping off his golden skin like a steel forge. He nodded at Gavin, who released her and stepped back far enough that she got a chill along her spine. Hannah's entire being trembled. Did she want the fantasy? Would it change anything, or just be a night that she would remember her whole life?

Brady closed the miniscule distance and cupped her cheeks with his big, work-roughened palms. His love for her shone in the milk chocolate depths of his eyes that always, *always*, made her feel like the most important person in the whole wide world.

The rest of the world fell away. Their kitchen, with the stainless-steel appliances and butter gray cabinetry. Even Gavin disappeared. She leaned into Brady's touch, feeling the holes in her heart fill and overflow. Her hands instinctually went to his bare chest. God, she loved his chest, with shoulders wide enough, strong enough, that she could lean on him, let him take her cares and worries away and be her bastion against the world. The tips of her fingers traced his solid, ripcord muscles.

Had there ever been a finer male chest? She didn't think so.

Brady murmured, "Hannah, babe, I love you and want to give you this fantasy. I know how much you love it when I use the cock ring with the attachment. Let me, let *us*, give you a night to remember."

He was serious. This wasn't a joke. She searched his gaze. He wanted to give her a threesome with another man.

Oh god! How could she say no?

She couldn't. The proffered forbidden fruit was within her reach, and she had learned the hard way that when opportunities presented themselves, she should grab them and run with them.

Brady traced her bottom lip with his thumb, tilted her head back some, and lowered his mouth. At the first brush of his lips over hers, she moaned in the back of her throat. Hannah gave herself over to Brady, the hot, demanding tangle of tongue and teeth seducing her, making her blind to anything but him. Brady kissed her and the rest of the world fell away. Always. From the first time he'd kissed her outside Giordano's after they'd shared a deep-dish pizza on their first date, to their last date at the club a week ago—he kissed her and she went up in flames.

She caressed his chest, trailing her fingers over his satiny skin. Yet before she managed to circle her arms up around his neck, he tore his mouth away. His chocolate gaze was black with lust. Then he swiveled her body in his arms and aligned her backside against his front. She could feel the firm ridge of his erection against her bottom.

Brady drew the red skirt of her mini dress up over her hips, causing the material to bunch at her waist. Beneath the skirt, she wore a matching red thong that was so teeny tiny, it barely covered her mound.

From this angle, she finally got a good look at Gavin. Where Brady was a blond golden Adonis with a close-cropped almost military style haircut, Gavin was shorter than Brady by an inch or so, and his midnight, chin-length hair was tousled, like he constantly ran his fingers through it. It was as if she had an angel on one side and the devil on the other. And his body—heaven help her. Miles upon miles of thick ropy muscle, the skin a burnished tan. His chest was covered in dark fur that funneled into a single trail that bisected his contoured abs and disappeared beneath his low riding jeans that cupped his parts. From the bulge straining the confines at his groin, he had a lot of cuppable parts. On his left shoulder and bicep, he sported a black tribal tattoo. She wanted to trace the inky lines—with her tongue.

Brady slipped his hand beneath her panties, delved between her folds, and grazed her clit with the calloused pads of his fingers. Brady knew what she liked, knew how to make her body sing from his efforts. Her being was engulfed in flames at his touch, at the prospect of both men loving her, of feeling all that testosterone surrounding her.

"Fuck, babe, you're so wet. I know you want this. Say yes. Then Gavin will fuck you while I watch. After that, we will both take you... together."

She moaned at the erotic image he was proposing. Brady swirled his digits around her nub. She canted her hips, needing more than the playful teasing strokes. He did this to her every damn time; sent her body up in flames like the Hindenburg in seconds, just from his fingers on her.

"Brady," she protested with a moan. The man knew how to take her body from zero to the brink of penultimate pleasure in two seconds flat. She should be embarrassed that she was exposed, that Gavin could see Brady's hand moving beneath her panties. She rocked her hips, canting them up for more as he teased her. And her gaze lowered to the hard bulge in Gavin's jeans.

Hannah licked her lips.

"Why don't you show Hannah what she will be missing out on if she says no, Gavin?" Brady commanded in his sex on a stick, bedroom voice that always turned her on. In this case, it added to the fire he was stoking with each swipe of his calloused fingers over her clit.

Gavin's gaze, which reminded her of budding leafy green

spring plants, smoldered, his attention directed at her crotch. And then he pegged her with an intense, panty-dropping stare. Their gazes clashed like a lightning bolt striking through her foundation. Hannah wondered if she would go up in a whiff of smoke as she spontaneously combusted from the heat.

"I think that's a great idea. Hannah, I've watched you every time you come to the station and this," his nimble fingers undid the fastening on his jeans and shoved his pants and boxers down to his muscular thighs, exposing his erect shaft, "is all for you. I can't help but get hard every time you're near. What do you think? You want this cock?" he asked, gripping his member. Gavin drew his fist up and down his length while Brady's fingers continued their frenetic rhythm against her pleasure button.

The erotic display was more than enough to lead her into temptation.

Hannah panted and rocked her hips, seduced by the tantalizing scene. She loved Brady, every inch of him, but next to him, Gavin had one of the best cocks she'd ever seen: long, thick, the bulbous head a few shades darker than the shaft, and with a pearly drop of pre-cum glistening on the crown. It was the most erotic, naughty act she had ever participated in. And that was saying something after having partaken in multiple scenes at Cuffs & Spurs with Brady. Hannah tried to remain firm, resolved to say no and pass on what was sure to be an alluring, pleasure-filled ride.

But—and it was a big, huge but—she would be lying if she said that Gavin did not fascinate her, tempt her with his wicked, dark yumminess. He did. Every time she visited Brady at the station, she had watched Gavin, with his soulful intensity. Secrets were shrouded in his gaze. And she'd wondered if he tasted as good as he looked.

Brady nuzzled the hollow spot at the base of her neck, nipping it and laving it with his tongue, never relenting as he played with her pussy. It was too much for her to resist. With each swipe of his fingers, another domino fell, eliminating her resolve. She felt Brady's approval and his need against her backside. This was turning him on, thinking about her with his best friend. That he would do this for her, give her this fantasy, made love for him swell in her chest. It loosened the death grip she held as the last domino fell, clearing the way.

"Yes," she finally sighed, wanting this, *needing* this night with the two big alphas like she needed air to breathe.

"Then get on your knees, love, and show me how much you want it," Gavin dared her, biting his full bottom lip, his gaze hooded as he held his dick, his hand stroking his shaft.

Brady pinched her clit and her pussy throbbed. "Do it, babe. I want to watch you take his dick in your mouth and your sweet pussy. But I get your ass."

Brady removed his fingers from her pussy, licked her cream from his digits, then gave her ass a hard swat. Gavin crooked a finger at her: the male equivalent of *come here, woman*. Hannah approached, her breathing erratic and pulse hammering in her veins. Gavin's magnetic gaze was like a tether, reeling her in. She stopped in front of him with half a foot of space between them—so close, she could feel the heat rolling off his big body —clenching her hands, with turbulent need humming in her veins.

She gazed at him, noting the day-old dark stubble lining his chin. This close, she discovered he had a tiny scar beside his left eyebrow and wondered how it had happened. His mouth was firm with a full bottom lip she wanted to suck on.

So why wasn't she doing it? This was her chance.

As if she were in a trance, her hands lifted. With the tips of her fingers, Hannah traced the defined lines of his pectorals, his flesh scorching her hands. Then, using his body for balance, she went up on her tiptoes. She stopped when her mouth was a heartbeat away from his, her gaze locked on his, their breaths mingling. Then Hannah traced his bottom lip with her tongue.

He had given her free rein until that point, making it her choice to touch him.

Gavin cupped her nape, tilted her head back and covered her lips with his. He plundered her mouth. The kiss took her body from zero to hot and heavy in under a minute. Why hadn't she kissed this man before tonight? That was the only thought she could drum up in her brain at the moment. He tasted like brandy and cigars and decadent sin. She mewled into the kiss and clung to him.

Hannah wasn't sure how he could kiss her right out of her head. Her brain clicked the *off* button. His hunger left her shaken and needy and wanting to climb him like a tree. Her body plastered itself to his and the proof of his desire pressed into her belly.

Gavin wrenched his mouth off hers, his face filled with dark carnality and potent yearning. He wanted her. Not just any woman, but *her*.

How had she never known? He'd hid his desire from her so well when they were all together.

And just like that, the last vestiges of her resistance slipped away because she saw the truth in his eyes. It was more than Gavin merely wanting a quick, hot fuck. He wanted her.

Desire she had held in check unfurled in her being. In this moment, tonight, she would give in to the fascination, the yearning she had denied she had for Gavin. To prove it, prove that she did want this with him, with them, she lowered herself to her knees before Gavin's impressive form. Gavin, a man she'd known as one of Brady's co-workers and closest friends. One she always considered a slice of beefcake she'd love to indulge in if she had never met Brady. And now Brady was giving her an all access pass?

She admired the six-pack abdominals and happy trail, hoping she'd get the chance to trace them with her tongue. Then she studied his shaft. He was beautiful. Hannah slid her hand around him and gripped his cock. His broad girth overflowed in her hand. The man wasn't just thick but long. He had a good inch or more on Brady's eight inches. She shivered, her pussy throbbing at the thought of feeling his member inside her.

Unable to wait any longer, she surrendered to the overwhelming desire flooding her veins. Leaning forward, her gaze on his face, she licked him from root to tip then swirled her tongue over the crown, lapping at the drop of pre-cum before taking him into her mouth.

At Gavin's deep groan, she purred. This was going to be a night to remember.

Chapter 2

F uck.

Watching his Hannah deep throat his best buddy Gavin in their kitchen was the hottest sight Brady had witnessed all week. Hell, all year. Brady knew exactly how incredible Hannah's mouth felt surrounding his dick.

Amazing. His woman loved sucking cock, and had a talent for it.

And the look of rapture on Gavin's face, like he had won the ultimate prize, was familiar too. Brady had witnessed a similar expression on his own face in the mirror when he'd taken Hannah from behind against the bathroom vanity just the other day. The entire tableau —with the backdrop of pristine granite countertops that Gavin had one hand on, as if to anchor himself and one cupped around Hannah's head, fingers threaded through her hair as she knelt on the burnished hardwood floor in supplication—had Brady's erection straining against the confines of his jeans. His dick was hard enough he could probably cut glass with the damn thing.

He and Gavin had topped women together before; plenty of them. They'd started during their senior year of high school when they'd both had the hots for Alice Johnson, and she for them. But never Hannah. From the moment he first met her, she'd engendered a possessive, protective beast inside Brady; the Dom in him had staked his claim upon her. Deep down, Brady knew it was because Hannah was special. He had plans—plans to marry Hannah and see his child at her breast. Since her advent into his life, Brady had done the unthinkable and cut Gavin out, not allowing him to top Hannah with him.

That made him a selfish bastard. He'd hurt his best friend. He knew that. When Gavin had tried talking to him about it, Brady had shut him out, which made him the biggest dick of the century. But with Hannah, she was different; he'd never felt that way about a woman before. It was like his soul had recognized his other half when they'd met. Like she was the missing puzzle piece of his life. He had taken one look at her in her classroom, surrounded by second graders, and had thought to himself: *it's her, there she is, finally*.

And he had acted out of character and kept her to himself because his entire foundation had shifted with that first meeting.

Before he asked Hannah to marry him, he had to mend his bond with Gavin. And he would do so by giving his best friend and his woman a night that they wouldn't forget. Plus, Brady needed to do this with Hannah because he needed to explain about his past with Gavin as a dual top. He prayed that, after experiencing a night with them, she would be less inclined to hate him for the omission. The truth was that he and Gavin had been dating women together for thirteen years before Hannah's advent into Brady's world. He hoped that, after tonight, Hannah wouldn't consider him a depraved asshole for failing to tell her about such a huge part of his life.

Brady hadn't intended to deceive her. But as time passed and they moved in together, the issue had become easier to sweep under the rug instead of facing it head on. It was cowardly, he knew that, and he hated himself for it. As for the fear slithering in his belly that she would leave him because of it, he forced it back, focusing instead on the desire burning through his body at the eroticism on display. It would all work out. Hannah loved him.

Brady wanted to give her this one night of uninhibited pleasure before he asked her to be his wife and told her the truth about his history with Gavin. And he wanted to give Gavin the night too.

Over the last two years, Gavin had sulked when it became apparent that Brady was not going to share Hannah. Their friendship grew strained because they had always shared women before. As they were both firemen, women were always throwing themselves at them. The pyro bunnies and firefighter groupies lined up in droves. It had been easy to entice a woman into a threesome with the two of them. Most of the women they bedded had sent him and Gavin off with a smile and a thank you.

Until Hannah.

She had changed everything.

She mewled around Gavin's shaft as she sucked him deep into her mouth. Gavin watched Hannah through hooded eyes, lust shrouding his features. But there was more in his expression as his hands cradled her head, his fingers laced through her auburn hair that always reminded Brady of tree leaves in the fall when they changed from green to burnt red. Gavin had feelings for Hannah that in his hunger, in his pleasure, he couldn't hide.

Brady sucked in a breath. He'd been a fucking asshole.

"That's it, babe. Suck him. Make him fill your mouth until there's no room for anything but his cock. Then I want you to swallow his come," Brady ordered. He undressed, shoving his jeans and boxers down his legs, and then stepping out of them. His erection sprang free of its confines. The tip seeped pre-cum at the tempting sight of Hannah's head bobbing up and down over Gavin's dick.

"She has a hot little mouth, doesn't she?" he said to Gavin.

"Like hot, electrified silk. Christ, just like that, love," Gavin said with a deep, rumbling groan.

Brady stood off to the side, getting the full view and observing Hannah's facial expressions, fisting his dick in slow, unhurried strokes as the sensual scene unfolded. Gavin was controlled at first. But Brady knew well the effects of Hannah's hot little mouth when she gave her all to sucking cock.

Gavin gripped her head and began fucking her mouth, his cock plunging with near brutal force. Brady knew by this point, Hannah's pussy would be dripping, she'd be so wet. He saw one of her hands snake down between her thighs and rub over her nub. He would put an end to that now.

"Hold up." He closed the short distance as Gavin withdrew from her mouth and Hannah whimpered.

Bending down, he removed her hand from her cunt. "You do not have permission to touch yourself. Tonight, this pussy belongs to me and Gavin. If you try to touch yourself again, I will spank that ass of yours. Understood, babe?"

"Yes, Sir," she mewled. Her eyes the color of the sky at midday were glassy with need.

"Good, proceed." He gestured.

"Actually, if we could move this into the bedroom... I'm craving a taste of her cunt," Gavin said with a low rumble and stared at Hannah with a look bordering on worship.

"What do you say, babe? Want to have Gavin eat your pussy?" Brady asked, lifting her up off her knees onto her feet. The sweet scent of her arousal hit him. It took everything inside him not to bend her over the counter and fuck her until his knees buckled.

Lifting her gaze to his, the cornflower blue orbs dark with her desire, she moaned, "Yes."

Her chest rose and fell with each panted breath. Her pupils were dilated, and she kept licking her lips.

Without another word, Brady hoisted Hannah into his arms. She had always fit there perfectly, like it was where she belonged. She slid her hands up around his neck, her fingers teasing the hair at his nape. And she latched her mouth against his neck, nuzzling him. For a moment, just one, he wanted to slam the bedroom door and lock the two of them inside, keeping Gavin out. But he breathed through the possessive, dominant nature she engendered in him, which demanded he hoard her away from all other men, and allowed the moment to pass. It was one night of sharing. Then his relationship with Gavin would be mended, and Hannah would know without a doubt that he would do anything for her.

When it came to Hannah, Brady was ultra-possessive, because no woman had ever mattered before like she did.

Inside their bedroom—which he'd given her free rein to decorate, where she had added small touches like the Wilson Hurley artwork on the walls and the snake plant in the far corner that filled the space with warmth, with life, just like Hannah— Brady laid her on the mammoth king-sized bed with its navy blanket and mounds of pillows. He couldn't help but admire the picture she made with her hair mussed, dress askew and breasts nearly spilling over the top of her costume.

Brady leaned over her, brushed his mouth over hers and commanded, "Strip for me, and lie on your back in the middle with your thighs spread."

Hannah shivered and nodded. He knew the expression in her eyes. It was the one that meant she was aroused to the point where she would do anything he asked. It wasn't any wonder she had such significance in his life, in his world. She was everything to him. Needing the connection, he tilted her face back, and slanted his mouth over hers. He swallowed her throaty moan, kissing her until they were both breathless and aching with need.

Brady tore his mouth from hers. He lost himself in her every damn time. There could be a five-alarm blaze and he could be the last firefighter standing, and one kiss would make it all disappear. She consumed him in the most delightful way possible.

"Damn, that was hot. I want a taste," Gavin said at his side. Brady glanced at him and a wordless understanding passed between them. They would play off each other until Hannah was writhing and screaming in ecstasy, and then they would claim her like they used to do with women: together.

Brady took a half step to the side and released Hannah just as Gavin drew her face his way and claimed her mouth. Hannah leaned in to Gavin, her moans muffled by his mouth.

When Gavin broke the kiss, he growled, "Do as Brady commanded, strip and lie in the middle of the bed with your thighs spread."

Hannah responded to Gavin's order with a nod, the perfect picture of submission. While she disrobed, Brady padded over to the nightstand, withdrawing the box of condoms and tube of lube. He opened the box for easier access and then strode into the bathroom to get a washcloth.

Brady strode back into the bedroom and sucked in a breath. Hannah looked like an offering to a god, splayed out on their bed. Gavin had shucked his pants and wasted little time climbing up onto the king bed. He knelt between her thighs, his hands caressing the front of her body, spreading her knees wider apart. Heat curled in Brady's midsection when Gavin positioned his face between her thighs and buried his mouth in her cunt. Hannah gasped, her back arched as Gavin ate her pussy with relish. Hannah's soft cries of pleasure filled the room.

Tantalized by the eroticism, Brady joined them in bed. He lay beside Hannah and began teasing her nipples with his fingers. She had generous, apple-sized globes, with dusky, large nipples. Brady glanced down as she writhed beneath Gavin's thrusting tongue. Gavin held her thighs open, lapping at her pussy like he'd finally tasted ambrosia.

Hannah did have the sweetest cunt. Lowering his mouth,

Brady curled his tongue around a pert nipple, laving and nipping the bud, letting her sweet vanilla taste roll around in his mouth. Her back arched, feeding him the mound. One of Hannah's hands gripped his head, holding him prisoner at her breast, the other was positioned on Gavin's head, her fingers clenched in his hair.

"Oh, god," Hannah panted and keened. Brady observed the play of emotions on her face. Passion exuded from her features. There was nothing lovelier than Hannah enjoying pleasure.

He released her tit with a popping sound and glanced down her supple form. Gavin's eyes were trained on Hannah's face and he looked… like a starving man finally being granted access to a buffet, like he had finally entered heaven and wanted to worship her. Brady knew the feeling.

Hannah's fingers slid down Brady's neck to his shoulders and dug in. Brady glanced back at her face, love swelling in his chest. She was the bravest person he knew. And she had no clue the gift she was bestowing on Gavin. He knew the moment she orgasmed. Her eyes glazed over. Her back arched. And her mouth dropped open on a long, keening moan.

"Ohhh, god, Gavin," she cried. Her body vibrated and quaked against him. She was so fucking gorgeous when she came.

But then Gavin rose and knelt between her thighs, holding out a hand toward Brady. Brady grabbed a foil packet and slapped it into Gavin's palm. Brady's cock jerked at what he knew was about to happen as Gavin sheathed his dick, rolling the latex down his staff.

Then Gavin gripped his cock with one hand and rubbed the head through Hannah's puffy, swollen folds before holding her hip with the other.

Fuck. Until now, Brady hadn't realized how much he had missed this over the past two years. Missed fucking a woman with his best friend. They looked at each other and Brady sucked in a breath, realizing how much he'd hurt Gavin by excluding him.

He was such an ass for keeping Gavin away. Perhaps if Hannah enjoyed being with them tonight, he could convince her to let Gavin join them more often. A wealth of understanding passed between the two men, and then Gavin was lining his dick up at Hannah's cunt entrance.

With the drops of semen seeping from his crown, Brady fisted his cock. He fucking loved watching Gavin fuck his woman.

Chapter 3

"Tell me what you want, Hannah," Gavin growled the order.

She lifted her gaze up until it connected with his and he groaned at what he saw. Hannah was aroused—for him. She wanted him. Hannah looked utterly gorgeous with her full lips swollen from their kisses and parted as she panted with desire. Her silken auburn hair was spread out on the pillow beneath her head. Her tits jiggled as she writhed, rotating her hips in her need.

"You, please. I need you inside me," she pleaded, canting her hips, trying to take his cock inside.

Gavin couldn't believe he was finally right where he'd longed to be. After all this time, Brady had lifted the moratorium and let him into bed with him and Hannah. Hannah of the sweet tits he still craved a taste of and an even sweeter pussy. He would have kept on eating her pussy if he hadn't been worried that he wouldn't last and would shoot his load all over the bedspread instead of inside her.

He'd dreamed about taking her; screwing his best friend's girl, the two of them, together like they'd used to do.

Through gritted teeth, need pounding in his veins, his cock straining to feel her heat wrapped around his length, he said in a low, husky voice, "Then you'll have me."

The caveman in him roared. His blood thundered in his body. Gavin gripped her lush, pale thighs, his gaze trained on her face, needing to watch her as he filled her up. Then he rocked his hips forward, plunging his cock in to the hilt until his balls pressed against her rear.

Oh, fuck!

A deep-seated groan rumbled in his chest. His eyes almost rolled back into his head. Her pussy clutched his shaft, shooting currents of unmitigated pleasure throughout his body, only to coalesce in his groin. Gavin nearly emptied his load, climaxing right then and there. He inhaled a breath and then another, computing math equations in his mind to corral his body back under his control. She made him feel like a teenager with his first woman.

Time stilled. Beads of sweat rolled down his back. The moment he felt like he had as much control back as he was going to get, Gavin moved, withdrawing until only the tip remained inside before sliding back inside, balls deep. Unable to help himself, he grunted, "Fuck."

"She's got a great pussy, doesn't she?" Brady said with a knowing glance, toying with Hannah's nipples as he watched the scene.

"Fuck, yeah." Gavin withdrew until only the head of his cock was sheathed in her gripping heat, before thrusting deep once more. Her back arched and her generous tits jiggled.

"Gavin," Hannah moaned his name like a prayer.

Hearing Hannah say his name in the throes of pleasure was all the encouragement he needed. Gavin didn't hold back, and unleashed his control. He couldn't hold back; he'd dreamed about this moment for far too long. Now that he felt her heat surround him, clasping his shaft to draw him deeper inside, he prayed he could last long enough to make it good for her, that he wouldn't finish before making her scream in ecstasy.

On his knees, he rocked his pelvis, setting a steady, pounding pace. As he gripped her lithe thighs, holding her open, the blissful expression on Hannah's face said it all, the way her bow-shaped mouth formed an O and she emitted the purest cries of ecstasy. But it was the way she writhed beneath him, bringing her hips up to meet his plunges that nearly drove him over the edge.

Using one of his thumbs, he circled her engorged clit as he pumped his cock in hard plunges. Her moans mingled with the slapping of their flesh. When she came, her tissues gripped his cock, spasming around his shaft, and his eyes did roll into the back of his head.

"Oh god!" Hannah cried, her body vibrating with the force of her climax as she jerked her hips.

That was when Gavin went primal on her sweet cunt. He leaned over her on his elbows and fucked her as if his life depended on it. She clung to him, her tiny nails digging into his back as he fucked her. Gavin lifted her legs up, wrapping them around his waist so he could plunge deeper. This close, her face was pure perfection.

At their side was Brady, watching it all. And then Brady turned Hannah's face toward him and took her mouth in a hungry, passionate kiss, and laid his other palm against Gavin's back. It electrified everything: the connection he'd been missing for two years since Hannah's arrival in Brady's life, in his life.

It was all it took. A bolt of lightning struck along his spine. His dick lengthened. His balls drew taut. He slammed home, Hannah keening into Brady's mouth as she climaxed again. He tossed his head back, straining.

"Fuck!" he bellowed as he emptied himself into her sweet heat. He thrust over and over again as tremors rocked his foundation. It was more than just back-buckling sex, he thought as he glanced down at Hannah and Brady, with Hannah's face one of sublime bliss, and Brady nuzzling her cheek. It had always been more than mere sex.

Chapter 4

Hannah was drifting in a semi-conscious, blissful state from her multiple orgasms. Her Christmas had taken a complete turnaround for the better. Her body was languorous and thoroughly satiated. The fragrance of their lovemaking—her and Gavin's—scented the air. She should be riddled with shame; she had screwed her boyfriend's best friend in a rather epic fashion. Gavin equaled Brady in his ability to take her right out of her mind and liquify her bones with euphoric pleasure.

The man had, to coin a phrase, fucked her brains out. And she had loved every naughty, delicious second of it.

Hannah sighed. She wasn't ashamed. It was just the oddest thing, how right it felt to bring Gavin into their bedroom play. And the thought of more erotic decadence, with him and Brady, turned her being inside out with unrepentant need.

She rested on her right side, sandwiched between both men on their California King mattress. Her head was pillowed on Gavin's firm chest, her left leg tossed across one of his muscular thighs as they recovered from the first volley of sensual indulgence, utterly sated. Her fingers toyed with the flat, brown disk of

Gavin's nipple, thrilling at the way it pebbled into a hard point at her touch. Gavin issued a deep rumble of approval at her caress that acted like a lightning rod of pleasure zapping through her system.

The fact that Brady had been there through it all, had encouraged each spine-tingling orgasm, settled any regret she might have felt. Brady's approval and the blatant desire he'd displayed when he'd kissed her while she'd climaxed around Gavin's thrusting shaft had made the orgasm burn that much hotter, that much brighter. For that single moment, the three of them had been intimately connected.

Brady's large, work-roughened hands skimmed from her shoulders down her spine to her bottom. He had such great hands. His touch sparked and sizzled along her spine.

"Mmmm," she hummed, canting her hips, craving more of him as he awakened her girly bits from their languid daze.

Brady palmed the globes of her rear. His familiar touch sent torrents of need rushing through her body. Brady rocked his erection through her crease. God, the man always, *always*, made her blood simmer, leaving her hot and bothered and ready for anything he had in mind. A single touch, and her body went up in flames.

"Brady," she moaned as one of his hands cupped a breast, pinching and tugging on her nipples the way he knew she adored, all while he teased her with his shaft. She wanted him inside her, now—so much so, that moisture leaked from her sex.

His lips and teeth grazed her neck. "Watching you with Gavin was hot as fuck, babe. But I know you want more, don't you?"

"Yes," she sighed, "please."

Brady chuckled darkly. "I know. I can feel how wet you are. Relax and let me stretch that pretty rosette of yours to take my cock. And then," he nibbled on her earlobe, "we're both going to fuck you."

"Oh god," she moaned with a gasp, because now that she knew what they each felt like inside her, she could vividly imagine the two of them at once.

Brady held her cheeks apart and slathered her back hole with lubricant. This wasn't her first time with anal. Brady had been the one to introduce her to the naughty indulgence shortly after they became an item. She loved it. Her eyes widened, and she gasped as he pressed a finger inside to stretch her. But then Gavin shifted to face her. His cock lengthened and pressed against her belly as he took her face between his hands and kissed her.

God. Just… god.

Hannah thought she already knew the meaning of sexual pleasure. These last two years, she and Brady tore up the sheets nightly, or really any other surface they could find. They had performed numerous scenes at their lifestyle club, Cuffs & Spurs. She loved that about him, about them, that after two years, the fires hadn't diminished but turned into an all-consuming, raging inferno. At some point, realistically, she knew it might diminish a little. But for now, she was going to take the offered pleasure with both hands and revel in it.

However, this—tonight, with two sets of firm male hands on her—was another level of ecstasy entirely. Gavin kissed her like his life depended on it. He dominantly controlled the tenor of their kiss, tangling his tongue with hers while his hands kneaded her tits. All that was happening while Brady plundered her ass, thrusting his fingers in and out of her forbidden channel.

Her world centered on the two big alphas as they turned her into a writhing mass of need. She moaned into Gavin's exquisite mouth when Brady added a second finger, thrusting deep. Gavin tore his lips from hers. She whimpered and opened her eyes.

Lust riddled Gavin's tan face. But he shifted and took one of her nipples into his mouth while his hand kneaded its twin, teasing the bud. Her hands slid into Gavin's thick head of hair, needing something to hold onto as she spiraled higher and higher.

Brady added a third and then a fourth finger, his fingers sawing in and out of her bottom. Then one of Gavin's hands teased her clit, circling the swollen bud again and again before he penetrated her pussy, thrusting two fingers in deep. Mewls spilled from the back of her mouth. Hannah stood on a precipice, with undiluted pleasure pounding through her body. It was a titillating foreshadowing of future events. The climax slammed into her system with the force of a rocket exploding.

"Oh god," she cried. Her back arched and her hips bucked as waves of ecstasy riddled her. She trembled, quaking, between them.

"There's more to come, babe. Let's get her into position, Gavin." Brady was totally the one in charge of tonight's decadent venture, she realized as he withdrew his fingers from her bottom. Then again, he was dominant in the bedroom. It was just enough dominance, and tended to melt her insides. Dominance in small batches, or in the bedroom, was super-hot. And while they were technically in a Dom/sub relationship, he wasn't a hard ass outside the bedroom.

Gavin released her breast with a pop and removed his fingers from her channel. He brushed his lips over hers before rolling onto his back. Gavin snagged a condom from the nightstand and rolled it down his thick length. Then, with Brady's help, he shifted her body so that she was straddling Gavin's pelvis.

Gavin's hands slid to her hips. Hannah braced her palms against his chest, working with him as he lifted her up, positioned his shaft at her entrance and then, with her gaze trained on his, she thrust down as he thrust up. He stroked in deep until he hit the lip of her womb. The man was just huge. She gasped as her body adjusted to his girth.

Once she was fully settled with Gavin's cock embedded in her sheath, Brady pushed her torso forward, positioning her so that she was flush against Gavin's muscular chest with his enigmatic face a scant inch away.

"Hey, beautiful. Deep breaths, and hold still until Brady fits his dick in your rosette. Your pussy feels so good, fluttering and clenching my cock, love," Gavin said, holding her upper thighs to keep her steady.

She curled her hands around Gavin's shoulders when Brady slathered more lube over her back entrance. Her breaths came out in a series of short pants; she heard the distinct rip of the foil packet and quivered. Two men at once. It was happening. Her deepest, darkest fantasy was coming to fruition because of Brady, because he loved her and wanted to give this to her. And Gavin too. She stared into his eyes and her heart tripped over itself. Before she had a chance to examine her feelings, the head of Brady's cock prodded her back sheath.

"Oh," she gasped, her fingers digging into Gavin's shoulders.

Brady gripped her hips. "Steady, babe. Let me inside. Deep breaths for me," Brady murmured the command.

She loved it when he became all authoritative and demanding in bed. Hannah took a deep breath and then another. Her eyes closed. Gavin was embedded in her pussy and unmoving as Brady pressed forward. His cock slid past the taut ring of muscle. Brady withdrew and thrust again, going deeper this time.

Oh! Sweet heavens! Rapture bombarded her. Dual penetration was the most incredible, mind-altering sensation. There was nothing like it. And it was different from having Brady use the cock ring with the dildo attached.

Brady rocked his hips over and over again, plowing deeper inside her rear with every stroke until he became fully submerged, with a deep seated groan. She had one cock in her pussy and one in her ass. Her body was electrified. It was as if every molecule were plugged into a super charged hydron collider, pumping nuclear fission levels of energy into her.

The three of them held still once Brady had slid in deep. They were connected. She heard their panted breaths at the exquisite pleasure of the moment. But she was ready for more, needed more.

"So, were you guys going to fuck me or is this a new way of cuddling?" she asked, her voice breathy and infused with need. She lifted her heavy lids and felt like she was drowning in jade.

Gavin barked out a rough laugh that was part groan, part chuckle.

Brady said, "See, told you she's rather demanding."

She glanced at Gavin's face and he gave her a smoldering look. "I think we should oblige her request. Her cunt's squeezing me so tight, I know I won't last long."

"Me either." Brady smacked her bottom with a playful strike before gripping her hips to hold her steady as he withdrew until merely the tip remained before slamming home until he was balls deep.

As he thrust in, Gavin withdrew, creating a seesaw effect, the two alphas moving in tandem, establishing a steady pace. All Hannah could do was hang on for the ride. And holy god, but it was more than she could have ever dreamed of. After all her wildest, wickedest fantasies, the reality didn't even come close—it surpassed them by leaps and bounds.

Brady drew her torso up until her backside was flush against his chest.

"Look at Gavin. See the way he looks at you, at the desire he has for you. Do you see it?"

"Yes," she moaned. She was entranced by the look in Gavin's eyes, at the emotions in their depths. He cared for her... maybe even loved her.

Her heart clenched, because deep down, she had feelings for him too. And she didn't know how to deal with those. She loved Brady. She couldn't have feelings for his best friend too. Could she?

Brady grazed her neck with his teeth. In his deep, bedroom voice, thick with lust, he murmured, "You like your gift? Being fucked by the two of us?"

Brady's hands slid up her torso and tweaked her nipples, rolling them between his fingers. Her gaze was heavy-lidded as she stared at Gavin as his abdominals flexed and he plunged deep inside her cunt. Then, with his thumb, he rubbed her clit in lazy circles.

"Yes, oh god, please!" she wailed.

Pleasure spiked and spiraled. The etchings of her release coiled in her belly. But the two men held her body hostage, keeping the pace at the perfect tempo to drive her out of her ever-loving mind.

"Please what?" Brady nipped her earlobe and thrust so deep, stars appeared in her vision.

"As much as I don't want this to end, we should let her come," Gavin said, flexing his hips and plunging deep.

Brady turned her face toward his. "Is that what you want? To come?"

"Yes, I… Brady, please." She was drowning in a sea of ecstasy, straining toward the glistening starlight.

"I love you, Hannah," Brady growled and took her mouth in a scorching kiss.

"I love you," she moaned when he tore his lips from hers and pushed her torso flat against Gavin's chest. Up close, as she looked into Gavin's eyes, she felt the same sentiment for him. But how could that be?

Gavin reached up, cupped her jaw, and gave her a deep, drugging kiss, like he could intuit the conflict raging inside her, could see the feelings that were bubbling just beneath the surface for him that she dared not let out.

He released her mouth. Brady leaned forward, over her back so that she was sandwiched between the two men, and they began to move together. They went slow at first, stroking their cocks deep inside her. One moment, she was so full she was overflowing and in the next, the pressure lessened as they withdrew.

But as they synced up, their tempo increased. Hannah lowered her face into the crook of Gavin's neck. She moaned and dug her nails into his chest as they proceeded to fuck her into the stratosphere.

"Oh fuck," Gavin groaned.

"See, I told you she was a great fuck."

"Her pussy feels like I plugged my dick into electrified silk," Gavin added.

"Her ass is just as tight," Brady grunted, his fingers digging into her hips.

Sweat slicked their bodies. They hammered her holes. Every atom in her body enflamed. With the next deep, dual thrusts, she keened, "Ohhh, god."

Hannah came. Hard. The climax blinded her. Ecstasy stole her breath. Tremors ripped through the fabric of her being. Her hips bucked between the plunging cocks. Her tissues gripped their shafts. Her climax set off theirs.

Gavin's cock jerked and he groaned, "Fuuuck."

"Hannah," Brady growled, pounding into her back channel as he came, his cock jolting.

Their hips rocked, sending little sparks of aftershocks through Hannah's body. She had never in her entire life felt as blissful as she did right now. Aftershocks rocked through her core. All three of them were connected. She could feel their pounding hearts, hear their breathing as they fought to regain a measure of control.

Sandwiched between them, she had never felt so safe, so sated, so loved.

And she wondered if she was going to be able to keep this feeling, or if it would dissolve in the morning light.

Chapter 5

S hit.

He'd told himself he wouldn't do it. That he could hold himself back. But he hadn't expected her to feel so right. Hadn't expect to feel pieces of himself he'd thought were lost forever slide back into place with the added sensation of fullness, of expansion as he sank inside her wet heat and felt like he'd come home.

How? How could that be?

Hannah rested against him, spooned against him in a hazy state of awareness. After the intensity of their lovemaking, Brady had been the first to break up the trio, flopping onto the bed beside Gavin while he had helped the semi-conscious Hannah off his lap. She'd curled onto her side, and he'd followed.

Gavin would follow her anywhere, even into hell. He would take whatever crumbs Brady would allow. Gavin cuddled Hannah. It was unbelievable, but he was still hard. Still desperate, and he craved the feel of her ass.

He breathed her in, that heady scent of vanilla, sex and Hannah. Brady rose, his gait unsteady, and trod into the bathroom, probably to deal with the condom. Gavin removed his own condom, tossed it into the trash by the nightstand and grabbed another. He needed to fuck her ass, to feel her rosette squeeze his cock.

He rolled the condom down his length, slicked his cock with lube and tugged her close. She sighed when he placed open-mouthed kisses against her neck, and shifted, arching against him like a sleek cat.

"Lift your leg, baby," he murmured by her ear.

Hannah didn't hesitate. And he moved that leg with her, positioning it over his upper thigh, granting him access to the crease between her legs. He positioned his cock against her stretched back hole.

"Gavin," she moaned as he fed his cock into the tight confines of her ass.

Gavin flexed his hips, pushing forward until he was balls deep. Jesus, hearing his name uttered with such need nearly unmanned him. Pulling her flush against him, he turned her head and took her mouth while he lazily stroked inside her ass. He snaked one hand down, rubbing her swollen nub, and pumped his hips.

He'd never thought in a million years that he would be here, with the taut clasp of her back channel clenching him, his name on her lips. When Brady had proposed giving Hannah a night with the two of them, he had jumped on the suggestion. And now, he worried even as he groaned into her hot little mouth with her tongue down his throat, that one night of being with her, with both of them, would never be enough.

That was why he was attempting to wring every ounce of pleasure he could from the night. If one night was all he was going to have with Hannah and Brady, he would damn well make it one that would live on and fuel his fantasies for years to come.

He felt the bed shift as Brady joined them once more. Gavin

lifted his mouth and stared at his best friend while he fucked his girl in the ass.

Brady's gaze took it all in, traveling down to Hannah's spread thighs, and darkened with lust.

"You like having Gavin fuck you, babe?" Brady fisted his dick.

"Yes," she moaned as Gavin stroked deep in her rear.

"I thought you might," Brady murmured and rolled a new condom over his length. Then he shifted, positioning himself at her front.

Gavin stilled his movements and felt the moment Brady entered her swollen pussy. Her ass tightened around his cock, squeezing his shaft and making his eyes roll back in his head. Brady looked at him over her shoulder and nodded, giving him the signal to take her out of her mind with pleasure. Brady shifted her leg—the one that had lain over his until he had joined them—up around his waist to give him better access to her pussy.

Hannah's sweet mumbled cries spilled from her mouth as they filled her holes. Together, they began a slow, steady campaign, thrusting into the woman they shared. This was what had been missing from Gavin's life these last two years.

Brady still had not explained why he'd shut Gavin out. But there was a part of Gavin that understood. Hannah was special. Hannah was the end of the line. She wasn't a casual lay or temporary diversion, not for either of them. Hannah was the real deal, the one to build a life with and make a family.

If Gavin were to wish for anything this Christmas, it would be that after tonight, they wouldn't shut him out. That they would welcome him back.

But he doubted even the merriment and generosity of the season would change Brady's mind.

BRADY FELT the link that had been missing these last two years slide into place. It made the sex hotter, more carnal, and more fulfilling. He'd missed taking a woman together with Gavin. And Hannah, judging from the rapturous haze over her features, was loving every minute as he and Gavin fucked her.

Gavin kneaded her breasts. Her mouth hung open, issuing a string of moans. Her gaze was half-lidded. And he felt Gavin stroke her back channel, felt him move through the delicate tissues, plunging his dick inside her. Brady's possessiveness reared its ugly head—the one that declared in no uncertain terms that Hannah belonged to him, and him alone. He hated that he wanted to snarl at Gavin, get him to back off.

Brady tempered his feelings. It was just for tonight. One night only, as a gift for Hannah. Because then, he was going to get a ring on her finger, make her his for all time.

Hannah's sweet cries spurred him on. Brady flexed his hips, his fingers digging into her sides, and pumped his dick in her slick heat.

Hannah clung to him. She was beyond the realm of pleasure and enjoying every minute of the double penetration. He had known she would. It was part of her makeup. She was the most carnal, open woman he'd ever been with, always willing to try new things. She reveled in her pleasure, gave herself over to it and submitted herself to his mastery, body and soul. She was everything a Dom could ever want.

He'd been the one to introduce her to anal sex and double penetration with a few of his cock rings.

He'd been the holdout, not wanting to share her with anyone, especially his best friend. And now he knew why as Gavin drew her face back and took her mouth in a hungry, possessive kiss. Because Gavin loved her too and, given time, could make Hannah love him.

Brady was a miserly old fuck and selfish to boot, and he'd not wanted to share her. It didn't matter that they had been sharing women for more than a decade by the time Hannah waltzed into his life. From the moment she did, he'd had the unwavering need to claim her for himself.

He tweaked one of her swollen nipples, getting a throaty moan from her as she ripped her mouth away from Gavin's.

"I need... oh. More, please. I'm so close," Hannah panted.

Brady nodded at Gavin. "I think we've played with her long enough. Let's give it to her."

Gavin scowled for a moment, a stubborn flare of rebellion in his gaze, before he finally conceded, "Let's do it. I want to hear you howl, baby."

Like they'd done hundreds of times before, they worked in concert, syncing their strokes, plunging deep. Hannah's arms wrapped around Brady's neck and she held on to him, buried her face against his throat.

His balls began to tauten, and Brady released his control, pounding into her sweet, clasping cunt with relish. He loved the way she felt around his shaft. And he could feel Gavin filling her, thrusting inside her, hammering her ass with hard, smacking thrusts.

"Oh, I... ahhh," Hannah keened, her hips bucking between them as she climaxed. Vibrations shook her small frame.

It began at the base of his spine, burning up his shaft like lava, before exploding like a volcanic eruption. Brady rammed inside her sheath again and again as he came.

"Hannah," he roared.

"Fuuuck!" Gavin grunted as his climax hit.

They drew it out for as long as possible, until the last drops had been expelled from his shaft. But he stayed with her, keep his softening shaft in her slick, quaking heat. Brady cupped Hannah's cheeks. "Look at me, babe."

Hannah lifted her lids, her gaze swamped with love and satiation. It was exactly as it should be.

Needing to claim her, he began, "I love you, babe. I hope you liked your Christmas present, but I have one more for you."

A delicate auburn brow rose, and she gave him a wicked grin. "More?"

Ignoring his best friend as he withdrew from Hannah's body, Brady shook his head and barreled on. He needed this, like an affirmation that even after tonight, she was still his, would always be his. "Not that, you naughty minx, although maybe later, after some sustenance. Another gift—or at least, I hope you will see it that way. I've loved you from the first moment we met. I will give you everything and anything to make you happy."

Hannah softened against him. "You do that already, I love you too—"

He cut her off by placing a finger over her lips. "And I wanted to ask you if you would do me the honor of becoming my wife? Marry me, Hannah."

Shock riddled her form for a second before tears slid from her eyes. And it was in her eyes he saw his future, saw the children they would make, and the life they would spend with one another. She reached for him, shoving his finger aside, and sputtered with smile, "Yes. Yes, I will marry you. Brady, I love you so much."

And she threw her arms around him.

He gathered her close, murmuring his love for her once more, but as he did, he glanced over her slim shoulder. Gavin lay supine on the bed, apart from them, staring at the ceiling, his face a mask of abject misery. It was Brady's fault. Once again, he'd dealt a crushing blow to his best friend, out of fear. And Brady wondered if he had done irreparable damage to their friendship. Now that she had said yes, even after tonight's erotic exploits, some of his doubts, his fears, waned.

Would Gavin ever forgive him for the way he had treated him?

But then Hannah kissed him, tugging his mouth down to

hers, and he let himself go into the beauty of her warmth, doing everything he could to ignore the elephant in the room. What should have been the happiest night of his life was tainted by his betrayal and mistreatment of Gavin. And Brady sincerely doubted there was any means of making recompense.

Chapter 6

The following morning, Hannah escorted Gavin to the front door.

"Are you sure you can't stay for breakfast? I make the best French toast. And I'm sure we could all use the calories after last night," she said, looking up at him.

It was almost too much, her kindness and giving heart. She accepted what they'd done in the dark of night without any regrets. He loved her. He knew he shouldn't, because she only had eyes for Brady. But he did. And now that he had been with her... he couldn't seem to stop his heart from rolling over and exposing its soft underbelly in her presence. "I wish I could. I'm sure the French toast is fabulous. I have to run home and then head into the station. Thank you, for everything."

Knowing it might be the last time he would ever get the chance to do this, he cupped her nape, tilted her head back and slanted his mouth over hers. She leaned into him, returning his kiss with equal fervor. He infused the kiss with everything he felt for her, hoping like hell it would be something she remembered even years from now.

Because he knew Brady. Brady had staked his claim on her, pushed up his plans to propose to drive home that she belonged to him. That Gavin was just a passing thought and act in their relationship.

Gavin kissed her until he felt her soften and surrender against him. Only then did he end the embrace, waiting until she lifted her gaze to his. "Thank you for everything, Hannah. I'll never forget it. I—"

"Gavin, is everything all right? You should stay and we can talk about it," she said, trying to soothe him.

Before he could say any more, Brady padded into the room, his hair still damp from the shower. Gavin shook his head. It was no use. Brady was shutting him out again. He brushed his lips against her temple. "Everything's fine," he lied. "Merry Christmas, and congrats on the engagement. I hope you two will be happy together."

And before she or Brady could respond, he pushed out the door. He had to get away. Now. Before he did something stupid —even more so than sleeping with Hannah last night—like confess his feelings for her.

He all but vaulted into his black Ram truck, gunned the engine, and tore out of the drive. Dejected, Gavin drove home. He had choices to make. If Brady was going to give him a taste of heaven only to cut him off at the knees and deny him once more, then he didn't think he could maintain their friendship.

They'd been friends since grade school. Brady wasn't just his friend; Gavin considered him his brother from another mother. And from that first time they'd shared a woman, they had become closer than brothers. They were both hetero and had no designs on one another in that way. But there was a completion that he hadn't found elsewhere.

Gavin had been with women in the two years since Hannah's advent into Brady's life and the moratorium Brady had enacted.

He was a red-blooded male who enjoyed the opposite sex. And as a firefighter, women tended to throw themselves at him. As a Dom of Cuffs & Spurs, the single subs lined up for a chance to scene with him. Yet not a single night had yielded more than a perfunctory release.

Until last night.

Gavin let himself into his house, heading straight for the shower. He could still smell Hannah's scent on him. It would drive him mad if he didn't wash it off, wash *her* off. He stripped as he walked, thinking he would toss the clothes in the wash before he left for the day. Erase all traces of her.

Because he couldn't think about her. Or Brady. Not if he wanted to retain some semblance of normalcy. In the shower, he let the hot water do its job, whisking away the tightness in his shoulders. He stood with his head lowered, palms braced against the tile wall.

The memories from last night suffused him. That first time with Hannah, when they'd all been connected, had been the most powerful orgasm he'd had in years. It had felt right, having a woman between them again. And Hannah... Jesus, he had it bad where that woman was concerned.

The thought of running into Brady every day, of seeing the satisfaction and the happiness on his face, knowing he got to go home to Hannah while Gavin stood on the sidelines hoping against hope that they would invite him back to share their bed, depressed the holy hell out of him. Hell, just knowing he was going to run into Brady at the station later that day made dread churn in his gut.

Perhaps he should put in for a transfer, go serve at another station. It would suck being the new man, lowest on the totem pole. But he would adjust. And he wouldn't have the constant reminder of what he couldn't have.

Deep down, he knew it was the answer. It just wasn't the one he wanted.

Gavin dressed for work, feeling like his heart was bleeding out while the rest of him continued to function like nothing was amiss.

Brady lifted a bite of Hannah's French toast to his mouth and sighed. God, could the woman cook.

"It's too bad that Gavin couldn't stay for breakfast. We have plenty," Hannah said, pouring herself another cup of coffee.

"I'm sure he had things to get done before he needs to be at the station later." *Not to mention, burn my name in effigy if the expression on Gavin's face was anything to go by.*

"Yes, well I… feel bad."

"Why?"

"Because I have you and he has no one. After last night," she sighed, "I just don't like to think of him at home alone with no one to make him French toast, is all."

Brady studied Hannah and the ring he'd slid on her finger. "That's because you have one of the biggest hearts of anyone I know." He clasped her hand in his and threaded their fingers together. "And I think he wanted to give us some privacy this morning, since you said you'd marry me."

A smile lit her eyes. "I did, didn't I? We haven't even discussed when or where or how big a wedding."

"Whatever you want. Just don't make me wait too long to marry you," he teased.

"How does the spring sound? Maybe June?" She rose from her seat, but before she could leave, he snagged her wrist and reeled her in, sliding his hands to her hips, pleased when she put her hands on his shoulders.

"June would be perfect. You're done with school. And we could find a nice place to go on our honeymoon like, say, Jamaica or Tahiti. Rent one of those cottages over the water."

He tugged her down onto his lap. She willingly entered his arms with love in her eyes and snuggled against him.

"It's too bad you need to go to work today. It would be nice if we could just stay in bed all day."

"True. But that doesn't mean I can't make the most of the time I have before I need to leave." He waggled his brows at her.

"But you have to go in like twenty minutes." She pouted, nibbling on her bottom lip.

"I can work with that. Let me show you." He needed to find reassurance in her arms. He stood, lifting her, and she issued a laughing squeak and clutched at his shoulders while he carried her into their bedroom, where he proved that he really could do a lot within twenty minutes.

LATER, in his truck on the way to the station, Brady tried to decide how to handle the debacle with Gavin. They needed to sit down and talk without anyone else around. Brady had to explain to Gavin that he'd not meant to hurt him—even though he knew that he had, that Brady had acted selfishly—and he wanted them, *needed* them to still be friends.

He needed to tell Gavin that, while they had shared Hannah last night, he didn't think he could allow it again. Not when he could see the feelings Gavin had for Hannah, and the abject misery on his face when Brady had proposed.

Brady pulled up his truck beside Gavin's, hoping they would have a spare minute. He needed to apologize for being a dick, at the very least.

Except the moment he walked through the door, a call came in: a three-car accident at a shopping mall. And from there, the day snowballed. The holidays could be the worst time of the year. People cooking feasts and not turning their stoves or ovens off properly. Not to mention the morons deep-frying whole turkeys on their back decks or porches. The department had had a few calls with people setting their houses on fire because of those.

The day flew by with call after call. Before Brady knew it, he was finally leaving, his shift having ended hours before. He and Gavin had worked together all day long, with Gavin giving him the cold shoulder and answering in single syllables.

By the time he stowed his gear, Gavin had already left for the day.

Brady sighed, climbing into his truck. They would talk. Perhaps he just needed to give Gavin a bit of space for a while.

Chapter 8

Hannah hummed in the kitchen while she stood at the stove. She was making white turkey chili with some of the extra turkey meat from their Christmas meal. Brady had forgotten to take some of the leftovers with him today, and into the pot they'd gone. Granted, he'd had to run out the door quickly after giving her three back-buckling orgasms, and a promise to return to her bed that evening and love her some more. She didn't know if he could love her more than he did. Between this morning's hanky panky and all the climaxes she'd experienced last night, it was a wonder she could function today.

And for the woman who had grown up with no one really caring whether she lived or died, Brady's love was a gift she would never take for granted. Hannah knew what it was like to go without. Perhaps that was what she recognized in Gavin: the same yearning need to be loved and accepted.

But that didn't mean she could love him too. At least, she didn't think she could.

She couldn't help but get a kick out of the tiny diamond winking up at her from her left hand. She and Brady were engaged. She could see it, their life together. She wanted babies with him—boys with his smile and girls with her eyes and then one day, if they were lucky, they would have grandchildren to boot. She wanted the whole enchilada.

Brady's love, his desire to build a life with her, continued to heal the emotional wounds Hannah carried around with her. It was like every day they were together mended another little piece of her heart.

But why wasn't she happier? Why was she struggling emotionally today? Physically, there was nothing wrong. Her body was still in blissed-out mode.

At the heart of it, she hated the way it had ended between them: her and Gavin and Brady. There was something there, something she couldn't quite put her finger on, that she was missing. She was thrilled at the thought of becoming Brady's wife. But there was a part of her soul that whispered: what about Gavin?

She'd loved being with Gavin last night and having him top her with Brady. Maybe she had liked it a little too much. Brady had likely sensed her overabundant enjoyment of the threesome. The man could get rather territorial sometimes, but she didn't mind it. It was one of the things she loved about him: that he took care of her, and always had her back.

But the solemn look on Gavin's face this morning had twisted her heart painfully. Hannah wanted to soothe him, to hug him, and give him back some of the joy he'd brought her last night. Because when she stopped for a moment and listened to the inner workings of her heart, she had to admit she had feelings for him.

Feelings she had no business having. She was marrying Brady.

What was it about Gavin that drew her in, besides the kinship of lost souls she felt in him? She knew what it was about Brady—that was easy. He made her laugh, they had similar tastes in movies and music. She didn't mind the hours he kept, most days.

He was the most honorable man she knew, brave and strong, and while he might get a bit dominant in the bedroom, he treated her like a true partner. He calmed her fears, let her lean, and treated her like a queen.

But what was it about Gavin? Other than that the man was sexy as hell, like a dark avenging angel. Hannah was drawn to his quixotic nature. Gavin exuded a steady, calm energy she wanted to absorb, whereas Brady was always in motion, laden with testosterone. When it came to Gavin, he was still a Dom—there was no doubt in her mind there—but he was one of those quiet ones. He reminded her of bedrock. He was reliable and firm. And he knew just how to kiss her.

The kiss this morning, the one he'd left her with, had made her want to sink into him and stay a while. She had feelings for Gavin. As much as she didn't want to, as much as she knew it was wrong of her, she did.

Dammit.

She needed more time; time to figure out how deep her feelings for Gavin went and if there was more to it with him. Hannah had no clue how to accomplish that, though. And it wasn't that she wanted to leave Brady or trade one Dom for the other, because she did not want that at all. She wouldn't have said yes to Brady's proposal if she did not love him as deeply as she did, and did not believe one hundred percent that they were meant for each other.

But then why did she feel like Gavin needed to be a part of it, a part of their relationship, included in it, even? Or was that just her way of wanting not just the cake, but the entire seven-course meal?

She turned off the burner and checked the time. Brady was late again. Maybe when he returned home, they should discuss last night over dinner. Because even though she hated to admit it, last night had changed the dynamics of her relationships both with Brady and with Gavin. They had cracked opened Pandora's

Box. And the problem was, now that she had tasted the forbidden fruit, she wanted more.

Could she and Brady include Gavin more often and have their relationship survive? Or would it dissolve into a jealous feud that left her alone and broken-hearted, and tore their friendship apart too?

Chapter 9

By the time Brady waltzed in through the garage door, Hannah had dinner ready on the table, an open bottle of beer for him, and a glass of pinot grigio for herself. She had bowls of the soup ready to go and had made warm sandwiches with some of the leftover turkey as well. She had a salad out on the table to make sure they got their greens in today.

Plus, they still had some apple pie for dessert.

A grin split Brady's face when he spied her and approached. She opened her arms, sighing with relief that he'd made it back in one piece. There was always that inkling of fear every time he stepped out the door that he might not come home. His job was dangerous. Hannah never forgot that for a second, which was why she tried to make sure that when he left for work in the mornings, they were never mad at each other.

Brady stepped into her arms, cupped her face in his hands and kissed her, long and deep.

"Missed you today," he murmured. "Sorry I'm late."

"I'm used to it by now, and don't mind. I'm just happy you're home," she said, nuzzling his neck, feeling safe and secure. "Are you hungry? I made some turkey chili and sandwiches."

"Starved. Haven't had a chance to eat today, with all the calls." He kissed her temple, then released her.

"Then eat. We have plenty more where that came from," she said, pointing him toward his chair.

"Have you started looking up dates so I can put in for the vacation?"

"Not yet. I was exhausted after you left this morning and went back to bed for a bit," she said sheepishly.

"Considering you're on winter break, I don't blame you. I know it's tough over the holidays with the hours I work. You have no idea how much I appreciate your understanding," he replied before taking a bite of the chili and moaning. "God, this is good. Have I told you today, how lucky I am to have you?"

"Yes, but I always like to hear it. You know, I recorded the game for you. Maybe after we've eaten, we could watch it."

He stared at her with an unreadable expression, then shook his head. "I don't deserve you." He took her hand in his and kissed the back of her hand.

"I figured you wouldn't get a chance to watch it at the station. If you want, you can call Gavin, have him come over, and the two of you could watch the game together," she offered.

"I don't think that's a good idea. Look, babe, there's a lot you don't know about Gavin and me," he said before shoveling another bite of chili into his mouth. He glanced away, avoiding her gaze. Inklings of doubt rose within her and slid fingers of fear about her neck.

"Then explain it to me. No secrets, remember? That was our deal from the start. But I get the feeling that I don't know the full story," she pushed, trying not to feel bad about the fatigue she noticed in his features.

Brady took a long sip of beer. His gaze cut back to her face and he grimaced. "You're right. There's something you should know. I should have told you before now but didn't really know how to bring it up. Last night wasn't the first time Gavin and I have shared a woman."

That was so not what she had been expecting that her breath expelled in a rush. A deep-seated part of her had worried he would ask for the ring back and say she wasn't what he wanted as a wife after all. "It wasn't?" she asked in a voice brimming with panic she tried to hide.

Releasing her hand, he shook his head and leaned back, his gaze unreadable. "No. Until you came along, we shared every woman we dated. In fact, we dated them together. It started when we were in high school and continued ever since. But you don't have to worry, it was just last night. If I stepped out of line and have made you uncomfortable, I'm sorry. That wasn't my intent. I wanted to give you the fantasy. Please don't be mad."

"I'm not mad. Although I'm not sure why you would keep this from me. Or why you decided that I'm not worthy of the both of you." They had dated women together until her. She loathed that her old fears—damn things were reliable—crawled their way back to the surface. What was it about her that made her unworthy?

Brady rose from his seat, moved around the table, and knelt beside her. He turned her in the chair until she faced him, and said, "Stop. It's nothing like that. From the moment I met you, Hannah, I knew you were it for me. That I wanted to spend my life with you, have kids with you, the whole nine yards. And because of that want, I also didn't want to share you. I love Gavin; he's my brother from another mother. But I wanted you for myself, and only for myself."

"Then why last night? Why dangle that carrot in front of Gavin and me? It's almost cruel."

"I was just trying to… shit, make amends with Gavin before I proposed. Why? Am I not enough for you now? Do you want Gavin instead?" he asked, his jaw clenched and eyes narrowed.

Needing to reassure him, she put her hands on either side of his face, the stubble of his five o'clock shadow bristled against her palms. With her heart in her throat, she said, "No, you are, I swear it. I love you so much, Brady, at times it overwhelms me. But I can't deny that I care about Gavin. He just looked so hurt this morning. And I don't want to come between you. If it means that much to you, he can join us again, I wouldn't mind. Especially if it's something the two of you need. Brady, I'm all in, no matter the form that takes."

Brady shook his head and jerked back, rising to stand. "I said it was for one night. That's it. I won't share you again."

"Okay. But please don't let it ruin your friendship. Not over me and this." She rose and slid her arms around him, searching his face. "Brady, I love you with everything I am."

His stiff form slackened. "I'm sorry. I didn't mean to snap. Gavin and I have some things to work out. I might ask him out for a beer tomorrow at Cuffs & Spurs so he and I can talk things over."

"It's all right." But deep down, Hannah knew it wasn't all right. Not with Brady, or Gavin—or her, for that matter, because she wanted Gavin too. She wanted them both, for keeps.

And she had no idea if she was going to be able to get it.

Chapter 10

"Gavin, hold up." Brady followed him into the locker room the next day. Gavin had seen Brady pull into the parking area, waving him down, only to turn on his heel and walk away.

Gavin was stowing his things in his locker by the time Brady reached him. Dread settled in his stomach. He swallowed it down. Gavin cast him a blasé stare, giving Brady no idea of where he stood. Gavin grunted. "What can I do for you?"

Gavin was going to make him work for it. Not that Brady blamed him one iota. This entire mess was all of his own making and he had a ton to answer for. Then he noticed the form in Gavin's hand; at the top, it read *Request for Transfer*.

Brady rocked back on his heels and felt like he'd taken a blow to his midsection. "You're applying to transfer out of the station?"

"Yep. I think it's for the best, don't you?" Gavin replied, shoving his backpack in his locker. He slammed the door shut with a loud thud that reverberated in the enclosed space.

Fury and fear had Brady snarling, "No. Screw that. This is

where you belong. As part of our station crew. Do you really want to go work with a team you don't know?"

"What *I* want seems to be irrelevant. I need time away to get my head on straight." What Gavin didn't say was that it was time away from Brady that he needed. It was there, written all over his face. Gavin shook his head in disappointment and turned to leave.

Before he made it out the door, Brady pleaded, "Look we can work something out. Don't leave like this, man."

Gavin rounded on him with a scowl creasing his brow. "I'm not going to settle for scraps. You're the one who decided to change things two years ago without considering me or my feelings on the matter. Work it out, to suit you? No thanks. I happen to love her too, you know."

"We can—"

Gavin snorted with derision. "The way I see it, there is no *we*. There hasn't been for two damn years. And I need to move on, for my own sanity, and I need you to let me. If you ever were truly my friend in the first place, do me a favor and just let me go," he said and strode away, leaving Brady staring after him.

The deepening pit of dread in Brady's stomach bottomed out. He had made a mess of things. He could see with perfect clarity where he'd gone wrong—from the moment he had met Hannah in her second-grade classroom, to their first date, and the first time he'd taken her to the club.

And he had no clue how to fix things.

———

GAVIN HESITATED on turning in the application. Folding it up, he shoved it in his back pocket as he got sidetracked cleaning gear. This time of year, with Christmas lights, firepits, and more to contend with, they tended to get more calls. He rose from his squat as the exterior side-door opened and in walked Hannah, carting two bags. She looked even better than she had the other night, which was saying something. Her auburn hair was down, her head covered by a knit gray cap in deference to the cold. She was bundled up in a puffy silver coat and wore skinny jeans that looked slicked on her gorgeous legs, and black boots that stopped just below her knees and made her legs appear even longer.

"Hannah, I didn't expect to see you here."

Her gaze roamed over his body. It might just have been a trick of the light or wishful thinking on his part, but she looked at him with desire in her eyes and something more that was there one second and gone the next. His gut clenched. She'd never know how much she meant to him. His heart ached because deep down, he knew he couldn't tell her. Brady might have been a dick and pulled the rug out from under him, but Gavin wouldn't take a bad situation and make it worse. Why he cared, he had no clue at the moment. Especially not when her sweet vanilla fragrance made need claw in his belly.

"Brady forgot his lunch again today and I wanted to bring it by," she said, her gaze never wavering from his, like she was committing him to memory.

But he wasn't the one she wanted; she wanted Brady. His heart sank as the tiny, minute sputter of hope died before it could breathe a single breath. "Oh. I think he's in the breakroom."

She held up the second bag in her hands. "I brought you some lunch too. You both work so hard, I…"

Touched, in spite of his aching heart, his hand closed around hers with his meal in it, and he felt her hand jolt and eyes widen. But not with shock—with heat and desire…for him. It was an unexpected gift, one he'd not expected this Christmas, to feel her desire and her care. Gavin fought back the urge to pull her into his arms and never let go. It took him a moment, because just touching her again, even doing something as innocent as holding her hand, was more than he'd thought he would ever have again. It took every ounce of strength inside him to do so, but he finally let go. And instead of doing what he wanted, he removed the bag from her hands. "That was very thoughtful of you, Hannah. Thank you."

"Gavin, I… I'm sorry if things got out of hand the other night. I hope you'll forgive me for the part I played. The last thing I want is you to be hurt. I know your friendship means the world to Brady. Please don't shut him out, or me. I know it's not how it used to be with you two."

His brows went up. "Brady told you? Everything?"

She nodded. "Yeah, he did. Give him time to make amends." And then she shocked him further by going up on her tiptoes and brushing her lips over his cheek. "You're a good man, Gavin, a good friend."

With a slight blush coloring her cheeks, she left him standing there, dazed and more than a little uncertain about the direction he should take. Was that what he needed to do? Be patient? He thought he had been, but perhaps he should hear Brady out. Maybe once they'd laid all their cards on the table, Gavin could decide whether to stay or transfer out.

He looked in the bag and couldn't help his smile. She'd even brought him pie.

THE CALL CAME in not an hour before his shift was scheduled to end. It was the story of Gavin's life. It was a two-alarm blaze in a warehouse a few blocks away from Main Street. Suited up in his BDUs, Gavin rode in the back of the truck with the captain shouting out orders.

After the team vented the roof, he and Brady would be the first two inside with the hose, with Brady on point. The warehouse had been a fixture in this town since the nineteen-fifties. By the time they reached the perimeter, the fire station from the north edge of town was already engaged. Flames burst and danced in the frigid temperatures, illuminating the blackened sky with an orange glow. Thick, dark smoke billowed from the roof.

At least the temperatures were holding steady above freezing. For now.

Their crew joined in the efforts as their captain took charge of the scene, calling out orders. The teams went up the ladders and started venting the building. Another team was charged with breaking out windows, opening the warehouse up to dispel the noxious gases so that his team could enter on this side, with another team from the other station entering on the opposite side. They were going to attempt a squeeze play to extinguish the blaze before it took down the whole building.

When the call came over the radio for their team to advance, Brady glanced at Gavin with a nod. In that moment, they buried all their turmoil with one another to do the job they were assigned to do. He might be pissed as hell at Brady and hurt over his handling of their friendship, but there was no one he would rather walk into danger with than him. Their cohorts, Jason and Tim, brought up the rear of their little party as they entered through what had been determined the best door. It was a side door on the building, away from where the flames burned hottest.

One by one, they filed in, breathing through the oxygen in their masks, holding the line as they dowsed flames in a measured, careful progression. The rush of the water, the distinct roar of flames, the reverberation of voices calling out orders and radio static, filled Gavin's head, along with the sound of his own breathing. They were making headway through what served as the offices for the warehouse, which were little more than half-walled cubicles.

Brady progressed forward, guiding the line. From the corner of his eye, Gavin noticed the ceiling to the right buckle in a line like an earthquake.

"Brady, watch out!" he shouted. Timber and plaster cracked, raining down in an explosion of gray dust.

Behind him, Jason and Tim yelled, "Pull the line back."

One minute Brady stood tall before him, in the next, there was a pile of debris on top of him with only his helmet visible. The world tilted on its axis and stood still.

"Firefighter down!" Gavin shouted over his radio. "I repeat, Tomlinson is down. We need paramedics standing by. Brady. Can you hear me?" Gavin inched forward, keeping an eye on the ceiling. When he was somewhat sure the rest of the building wasn't going to come crashing down on their heads, he bent near Brady and started hefting debris. Jason and Tim were there too.

"Jeffries, what the hell is going on?" Chief O'Rourke's voice came over the com.

Lifting a chunk of the ceiling off Brady's still form, Gavin replied, "Part of the ceiling collapsed, Chief. You need to send in another team in the other entrance. And we need help getting Tomlinson dug out."

"Is he alive?" Chief asked.

"I don't know yet. We need help in here. Over." He ignored the rest of the orders as he worked to free Brady's body. They became background noise to his own labored breathing as he fought not to panic.

Don't be dead. Please, don't be dead.

The mantra repeated itself in his head again and again. There was a buzzing in his ears. The entire scene took on a surreal bent. He kept eyeing the ceiling as they worked to dig him out. Gavin had no idea how long it took them to clear away enough debris to extract Brady from the rubble. It could have been minutes or hours. Time felt suspended and he found himself praying to whomever would listen that Brady would make it out of this. A pair of paramedics had entered behind them with a backboard between them. He knew Mindy and Rick. They were a solid pair. As a group, they secured Brady to the backboard, worried that they could paralyze him if something was broken that they didn't know about.

"On three," Rick shouted above the din.

And on three, they shifted him, secured against the backboard and rolled him onto his back.

"I've got a pulse," Mindy said, her fingers on his neck. Then she ordered, "Let's get him outside. Then we can get his helmet off and into the waiting ambulance. On my count."

Gavin almost sagged with relief. Brady was alive. He was out cold beneath the mask, and blood coated his shoulder, but he was alive. Thank Christ!

Brady moaned in agony as they carted him out on a backboard and loaded him onto a stretcher. Mindy and Rick worked in concert, getting his helmet off, checking his vitals. They found a puncture wound on his shoulder that they packed with gauze to stop the bleeding while they transported him to the hospital. With Gavin's help, they removed his jacket to patch up the wound, and started an IV.

When they no longer needed his aid, Gavin stood there watching as they loaded his best friend onto the waiting ambulance.

"Are you coming?" Rick shouted. "We need to get him to the hospital now."

"I'll follow you. Get going. Take care of him."

Rick nodded as he shut the door. "We will."

The ambulance sirens blared to life. People and vehicles moved out of the way as it left the scene. Gavin watched the rear lights as they disappeared around a turn. Brady was alive, but they had no idea how bad his injuries were, and he… *Jesus*. He swiped a hand over his face. He couldn't lose it. Not here. And not now.

He had to go tell Hannah. He'd rather stand before a firing squad than tell her Brady was hurt. But it was what Brady would want; he'd want it coming from Gavin and not someone else.

Captain O'Rourke sauntered over with a scowl on his face. It seemed to be a permanent scowl, given the deep grooves in his forehead, and matched the downturn of his lips. "What the fuck happened?"

"Part of the ceiling collapsed. He couldn't get out of the path fast enough. It happened so quick, the damn ceiling exploded."

O'Rourke nodded. "I've seen it happen before. But it's fucked up that it happened to one of mine." He gave Gavin a head to toe assessment. "You're off duty. We have the coverage, and the fire is under control. You follow him to the hospital and check in; give us updates until the rest of us can get there."

Gavin grimaced. "I have a stop to make on the way. His fiancée needs to know."

"Fiancée? I didn't know he'd gotten engaged," Captain O'Rourke said with a shake of his head and what looked like the weight of the world on his sagging shoulders.

"Brady proposed at Christmas and she said yes. I need to go get her, tell her what happened, and get her to the hospital."

"Fuck, all right. Take my pickup back to the station. I'll catch a ride on the engine." The captain nodded, handing Gavin the keys.

"Will do, Captain. I'll leave it at the station for you." Not wasting any more time, Gavin strode over to the large white truck with the fire department emblem emblazoned in red on the doors. He removed the harness with the oxygen tank, and his breathing apparatus. He stowed those in the passenger seat and took his helmet off, adding it to the pile.

Then he finally climbed into the cab. He flipped the sirens on, left the scene and drove like a man possessed. Jackson wasn't a large town by any means. Some days, he hated its small size, and on others, like today, he was never so happy to live in a small city. He arrived back at the station in record time. He didn't even stop inside the firehouse for more than a moment to drop off the captain's keys and deposit his breathing apparatus, tank, and

66

helmet. He would clean them and do a thorough check on his equipment later, once he knew that Brady was going to pull through. Grabbing his backpack with his change of clothes from his locker, he carried it with him and tossed it in the back seat of his truck.

He would change at the hospital and worry about the rest later. But first, he had to go tell the woman he loved that her fiancée was in the hospital, that he'd been hurt on the job, and they didn't know how badly yet.

Chapter 11

Hannah answered the door, trying to think of who could possibly be visiting at this time of night. It was frigid out, with temperatures forecasted to dip below freezing again tonight.

She yanked the door open and felt her heart drop. Gavin stood on the front porch, illuminated by their Christmas lights.

"Gavin, what's going on?" she asked, because he was still dressed in his gear. It made her gut clench to see him on her front stoop in his firefighter jacket and pants, staring at her with a solemnness that was like the Grim Reaper walking across her grave.

Her heart thumped wildly in her chest. The spaghetti she had eaten for dinner threatened to crawl back up her throat.

Gavin approached and grabbed her hands. Hannah's knees wobbled.

"Gavin? What are you doing here? Where's…" That's when she knew. Her heart sank into her toes as she searched his face.

"I'm so sorry to be the one but—"

"Please tell me he's not…" He couldn't be dead. They were

just starting their life together. She'd called her girlfriends today to tell them about the engagement. It couldn't be over.

Gavin shook his head in the negative, his jade eyes glowing with intensity. "No, he's alive. I don't want to scare you. He was hurt in a blaze, badly, and is at the hospital."

"Then what are we waiting for? We need to go. We need to be there," she replied, disentangling her fingers from his. She grabbed her coat, slid her boots on, and remembered—just barely—to grab her purse and house keys. Her mind raced. How bad was bad?

"I'll drive. Come on," Gavin said, patient as ever, ushering her to his truck.

Hannah's legs resembled pudding at this point. She put one foot in front of the other with sheer determination. Gavin lifted her up into his big black truck then strode around the hood to the driver's side and vaulted in. The engine roared to life. Gavin glanced at her.

"Deep breaths, baby. Not to worry, he's too ornery to die on us," he reassured her. His words broke through the fear thundering in her body.

"Us?" she whispered, her throat tight, and regarded him, fighting back the deluge of tears threatening.

In the dim dashboard light, his handsome face softened, and he nodded. "Yeah, us."

She reached for him, grabbed his hand and threaded her fingers through his. "Us," she repeated, feeling her heart swell with hope—and more.

Gavin lifted their clasped hands and brushed his lips over the back of her hand. "I will be there for you and for Brady, no matter what. I love you both."

It was all there in his eyes, turned liquid silver in the dim light: everything he felt for her, naked and on display. She swallowed the lump in her throat. Hannah didn't know why she'd never seen how much he cared for her before.

Yes she did, dammit. Because she hadn't wanted to see it. She hadn't been ready to admit her feelings for him. And she still wasn't sure that Brady would be all right with her feelings for his best friend. A few tears slid down her cheeks. She loved Gavin too.

Why did it have to be so complicated?

She didn't know if she could admit her feelings for Gavin and keep both men. It made the words stick in her throat. Gavin brushed his lips over the back of her hand again, not pressing her to reply, before he lowered their hands. But he didn't release hers and kept her hand clasped in his larger one, feeding her his strength and support. Then he backed out of their driveway. Speeding through the late-night streets, Gavin drove as confidently as Brady.

They screeched into a parking spot in front of the hospital. Only then did Gavin release her hand, just long enough for them to emerge from his truck. But once outside, again, he clasped her hand and led her into the emergency waiting room.

The waiting room was half full. Many of the people were coughing. She knew this time of year was high flu season, with all the people traveling.

Gavin located a few empty seats away from the crowd. "Have a seat. I'm going to check in, see if they can give me any information on his status as one of his crew."

"Thank you, Gavin," Hannah said, giving his hand a firm squeeze before releasing it. Then she sat in one of the chairs. Her legs were still doing an imitation of pudding, anyhow. If not for Gavin's strength and a driving fear to know whether Brady was okay, she doubted she would have made it here on her own.

He left her there for a few minutes while he went up to the nurse's station. Looking at his back, at the tension in the lines of his body, Hannah realized with perfect clarity she had to tell him how she felt about him. Today was living proof that waiting to tell a person how you felt about them was stupid and irresponsible. In a blink, everything could change. And what if it had been Gavin injured, or worse, and she'd not told him? The regret would have eaten her alive.

Gavin turned and headed her way, his face shrouded in secrets. She had once asked Brady how he could see some of the things he did—the fatal accidents and human suffering—and not let it get to him. He had told her at the time that he compartmentalized while he was working. They all did. It was only afterwards that he allowed it to sink in. And from Gavin's expression, she had a feeling he did the same thing. On top of that, she'd hurt him by not giving him the words back when he had come to her, to make sure she was here, and given her his strength to lean on and more.

He sat in the seat beside her.

"Anything?" she asked, on edge with worry for Brady.

"They're working on him right now. The good news is that he's conscious. Bad news is he's going to be like a constipated bear being out of work on medical leave while he recovers. They can't tell me all his injuries yet. But he's alive, and is going to pull through this."

She sagged with relief, blinking back the rush of tears. Brady was going to live. He would recover—if she had to push him, nag him to do it, she would.

Riding high on a wave of pure emotion, she cupped his cheek with her palm. "I love you, Gavin. I know I should have said it back in your truck. The thing is, I love you both. I don't know how that works in the real world. And it scares me every bit as much as one of you being injured or worse."

Gavin's gaze smoldered with warmth and love. He kissed her palm. "Don't worry about that right now. We'll get it sorted."

And then he put his arm around her shoulders, letting her rest her head against him, being her rock, and something inside Hannah clicked into place.

They were meant to be together. The three of them. She had

no idea how the logistics would work—she just knew it, felt it. That was why the other night had been so seamless. They fit.

Throughout the long hours waiting for word, waiting to be allowed in to see Brady, Gavin was there for Hannah. He was her shoulder to lean upon and bastion against the fear. And she very much doubted she would have made it through the intermittent hours, even with the other firefighters from his unit and members of their club showing up, until they were let back into Brady's hospital room—without Gavin at her side, feeding her his strength.

Chapter 12

Brady emerged from a fog to find Gavin sitting on the small couch in his hospital room, his head lowered to his chest in sleep. On his lap was Hannah—or, more accurately, her head was pillowed on his lap as she lay supine on the couch, covered with a hospital blanket.

Brady shifted, mindful of his immobile arm and all the machines he was hooked up to, the movement so slight, it barely stirred the air. But Gavin was used to sleeping light, always at the ready because of their job, and lifted his dark head.

Gavin stared at him across the small expanse. And Brady knew how close a call he'd had today. So did Gavin. And there was a wealth of things Gavin wasn't saying that Brady already understood with perfect clarity.

He'd come close to dying while trying to deny that they were a unit. The three of them, together, just fit. Brady did not understand the whys of it, why there was nothing that felt truer than being with Hannah together, screwing her together, loving her together.

"Gave us quite the scare," Gavin murmured with a raised brow.

"Sorry about that. How bad is it?" Brady's voice sounded distant and gruff, even to his own ears. He'd passed out from the pain after he'd woken up in the emergency room.

"Fractured left forearm, a concussion, and there's a puncture wound on your left shoulder they had to do surgery on and stitch up. Could have been worse." Gavin's voice had Hannah's eyes snapping open.

Gavin glanced down at Hannah with a look Brady was all too familiar with; the man was thoroughly besotted with her. It was hard not to be, and he knew that well because he looked at her the same way: like she was his whole world.

"Look who's awake," Gavin murmured gently, stroking a hand over her head.

And, wonder of wonders, Brady's normal knee-jerk possessiveness was absent. Granted, it could be due to the morphine. But deep down, he understood it was because he was finally okay with sharing her with Gavin—as it was meant to be, as it should have been from the start.

Hannah shifted and glanced his way. She let out a little sob and sprang up from the couch, almost wiping out on the blanket as she dashed to his side.

Tears fell down her cheeks as she leaned over and cupped his face in her hands. "You scared the crap out of me."

He smiled against her palms and rubbed his face against them. "I know, babe. I'm all right, I promise." Careful of the IV in his right arm, he brought his hand up and gripped hers, kissing her palm.

"Is there anything I can do?" she asked, searching his face like she wanted to stitch him up herself.

"Yeah, there is," Brady murmured, noting that Gavin stood up, still wearing his uniform pants.

"Anything," she swore.

"Kiss me," he demanded, because there had been a moment as the ceiling had collapsed in on his head where he had thought:

this is it, the end. And the only thing he'd wished for was to kiss Hannah one more time, and to make things right with Gavin.

Hannah leaned forward and brushed her lips over his. He could taste the salty flavor of her tears and her unique flavor, which declared her his woman. But, in truth, she was *theirs.* He couldn't shut Gavin out anymore, and hoped like hell Hannah would be okay with it.

If not? Shoot, he had no idea. Only that he and Gavin would work it out, somehow.

Brady slid into the kiss, returning it as much as he was able to since he was immobile and could do little more than lift his head. He poured every ounce of his love for her into his kiss, praying that this mishap wasn't enough to scare her off.

Hannah tore her mouth away from his, panting from the exchange. Even in his morphine-induced haze, pride enveloped him. Yeah, she still wanted him. While they had been occupied, Gavin had moved over and now stood at her side.

Brady began, his words a bit slurred as he fought the effects of the drug, "Hannah, babe, I need to ask you something before the drugs make me too drowsy and I forget. But I need to know if you have it in your heart to love us—both of us. Gavin and I are a team, and I need to know that you're okay with that, with including him in our lives, with—"

"Stop. Brady," she put her fingers over his mouth, "I don't know how it will work. How it could. I know that I'm not supposed to love you both, that I will be viewed as a pariah, but I don't care. I love you both and plan on keeping the two of you."

The light kicked on as Brady looked between them: Gavin's arm around Hannah's waist, the familiarity and ease between them. "You guys already talked."

Gavin wore all his emotions on his face as he glanced at Hannah before turning his gaze back toward Brady. "We had the time while they were patching you up. But yeah, she's ours, Brady, never fear. We were just waiting for you to catch up."

"Is that right?" Brady murmured, feeling his soul settle back into place. They were a unit, the way it was always meant to be. And the guilt he'd felt diminished some. He still had a lot to make up for, to Gavin and Hannah, for the way he'd bungled things. But they would get there, eventually.

"Yep. And don't you forget it, mister," she said, squeezing his uninjured hand.

"I won't," he swore, "not now, not ever. We're in this together." Brady sighed, his eyes closing as a new infusion of morphine flooded his system.

"Yes, we are. Now get some sleep. We're not going anywhere," Hannah ordered.

"Bossy! See, it's going to take more than one of us to keep her in line," Gavin teased.

"Yeah, but she still needs to marry me," Brady said, the undertow pulling him down.

"I will. Once you're healed up, you big lug," were the last words he heard before he drifted off into Neverland.

Chapter 13

New Year's Eve

The plan for the night was all set. They'd been caring for Brady around the clock since he'd been released from the hospital three days ago. Hannah had carried the brunt of it more than Gavin, since she was off for winter break while Gavin worked his shifts at the fire station before coming back each night to help her out, thank goodness.

Gavin had been correct when he'd said Brady would end up acting like a constipated bear while he recovered. Difficult had been an understatement. But it stemmed from his inaction. Brady was a man of action, and not having an outlet for all the energy, even banged up as he was, was tantamount to torture for the man. He was resting in the bedroom, watching television, and Hannah had just the remedy to get him out of his funk: sex, and lots of it. Brady wouldn't have to do any of the work, either. He could just lie there while she did it all—as long as they didn't jostle his left arm or shoulder, he would be good.

But to help her out, Gavin had the next forty-eight hours off from the station and they were going to make the most of it. Not that she and Gavin hadn't had sex while Brady was down for the count—with Brady's blessing, of course. Because they had, all over the house. The man had taken her in the shower and at the kitchen table. Up against the wall in the living room. He was a singularly gifted lover. Just this morning, over breakfast, he'd pulled her onto his lap and had his merry way with her.

But tonight, they were going to include Brady. The man was being ornery and was a rather bad patient. While he couldn't move much and was flat on his back per doctor's orders, a few days had passed, and the best way to get him past the hump of inactivity was, well, to hump his brains out. And he wouldn't even have to do anything but lie there in bed and take it.

Gavin was going to be a part of it. Hannah turned to him in the hall. The man had been her rock while Brady recovered.

"Are you ready?" she asked. Her belly quivered at his seductive smirk.

"For you, always," Gavin murmured, sliding an arm about her waist.

"Now, I might need your help to make sure we don't accidentally hurt Brady." The one thing Brady didn't need was more medical leave. The man would drive her to drink then.

"Not to worry, I won't let anything bad happen." He pressed a kiss on her mouth. It was meant to be chaste, nothing more than a brushing of their lips together. But she couldn't help herself with Gavin—or Brady, for that matter. Kissing either man made her world align and caused everything else to disappear but the guy kissing her.

She was the one to end it and ripped her mouth away, breathing heavily. "Sorry, it's not that I don't want to keep kissing you, but if we keep that up…"

"I'll end up fucking you in the hallway instead of with Brady?" he teased and tugged on her ponytail.

"Yeah. I can't help it. One touch, and I'm a goner."

"Just what every man wants to hear from his woman: that she

is helpless to resist." He waggled his dark brows in a dramatic fashion.

"Let's go, I can't wait any longer." She couldn't. Not with the way her body electrified at his touch, and her need to taste Brady. Today would be an affirmation of life—of Brady's life, and their lives together.

They entered the bedroom where Brady was stationed on the bed, his left arm in a sling. He was wearing a pair of gray sweats that rode low on his hips, and the television was playing some game on the sports channel.

Brady turned his head at their entrance. "What do you know, the peanut gallery has arrived. You look quite determined, Hannah, everything all right?"

That was when his gaze dipped to her fluffy pink robe. She didn't have a stitch on underneath so that they could get right to the point.

"Everything's perfect." She unbelted the robe and let it slide to the floor. Brady sucked in a breath. The front of his sweats began to tent.

She knew he needed an orgasm or two. Gavin padded over to the nightstand, pulling condoms and lube from the drawer.

"What's going on?" Brady asked, his voice strained.

She could tell he was trying not to be aroused and was failing in that regard. "What does it look like? We're going to fuck, the three of us."

"I can't—"

"Sure you can. You won't have to lift a finger. Just lie there, and I will handle all the rest. Gavin, help me get his pants off, will you?"

"Certainly," Gavin remarked and tugged his shirt off quickly, tossing it aside.

It took the two of them to undress him, with Gavin lifting Brady up a bit while Hannah pulled his gray sweats down. As she had suspected, there was a part of him that was really happy they were doing this.

Once Brady was naked, Hannah took in his injuries, and climbed into bed with him. She straddled his legs, and ran her hands up his muscular thighs until she encountered his shaft. Sliding a hand around the base, she squeezed.

"Oh, fuck, that feels good," Brady hissed.

"I thought you'd like that. Now, the rules are, if you are in any pain, you tell me—us—and we will stop," Hannah said, bending down to run her tongue over the crown. She inhaled his scent and purred.

"Like I'm the submissive one?" Brady said with a moan.

"Exactly like that, dude. Let her suck you off. Our woman is particularly skilled in that arena," Gavin said from behind her.

Tendrils of heat curled in her belly as Gavin climbed into bed behind her and massaged her bottom.

"Don't I know it. I'm at your mercy," Brady grumbled.

She looked up at him through her lashes, her hand sliding up and down his shaft in delicate strokes. Brady's gaze was trained on her as she licked his crown like he was her favorite lollipop before she opened up and took him inside, sucking the head and then the rest of his shaft into her mouth.

Brady let out a deep groan. "Jesus. Whatever you do, babe, don't stop."

She didn't plan on it. In response, she sucked hard on his shaft, drawing a deep-throated moan from him, and then continued stroking his shaft with her mouth.

Gavin's hands spread the globes of her rear, and his tongue swiped through her crease. She moaned around Brady's cock as Gavin ate her pussy like it was a delicacy. Gavin was particular skilled at oral. Last night, he'd spent a good thirty minutes eating her out. She'd come so many times, she was delirious by the time he finished. His tongue plunged inside her and she gasped. Her moans garbled around Brady's shaft as she swallowed his length.

"I want to watch you fuck her," Brady said, a hint of steel in his voice, his dominance rampaging back to the forefront.

Gavin's mouth left her sex and he growled, "I can do that. I can't wait any longer to feel her cunt."

"You just fucked her this morning. I know, because I could hear you in here," Brady grumbled.

"She tends to bring it out in me. The need to always be fucking her," Gavin remarked and the head of his cock pressed against her entrance.

"That she does. I understand the sentiment well. That's it, babe. I love your hot little mouth on my dick," Brady gasped, his stomach muscles flexing as she took him down deep.

Gavin clasped her hips and, in a single thrust, embedded his shaft in her pussy.

"Mmm," she moaned around Brady's cock. Hannah forced herself to concentrate on Brady in her mouth and not the cock currently stroking inside her sheath.

Gavin pounded her cunt, his pace fast and furious, driving her body up a precipice of desire that left her shaking and quivering for more. Her body coiled higher, tighter, as she tilted and tossed her hips back for more earth-shattering lovemaking.

"Babe, stop. I don't want to come in your mouth," Brady commanded.

She released his cock with a popping sound. "But Brady, I want… you need." She panted, her eyes rolling back in her head at Gavin's hard, ramming thrusts in her pussy.

"I know what I need. I need to be inside your pretty cunt while Gavin fucks your ass. I want to come inside you," Brady said with a guttural groan.

She whimpered as Gavin withdrew his shaft. "Oh god, okay, just hurry. I need you both."

"Let me get you situated, love," Gavin murmured, shifting her body forward until her pussy was hovering over Brady's cock.

She took a condom from the nightstand and rolled it over his length. With Gavin's hands on her hips, she thrust down, taking Brady inside, and moaned. Then Gavin pressed her torso forward. She propped herself up on her hands, mindful of Brady's shoulder and left arm. Gavin slathered lube over her rosette, pressing one finger inside and then another, stretching her before replacing his fingers with his dick.

She held still, breathing deeply while Gavin fed his cock into her ass, staring down at Brady, feeling more love than she'd ever dreamed was possible. She mewled in the back of her throat.

When both of her men were buried deep inside her, Hannah knew in her heart of hearts that she was the luckiest woman on the planet. She had not one but two honorable, sexy men who loved her like no other.

And then she and Gavin began to move, making sure that Brady stayed as immobile as possible. Hannah had to focus or she would lose the rhythm because they felt so good. There was nothing in the world like double penetration. As she stared at Brady's handsome face, at his heavy-lidded gaze infused with lust and love, he rocked his hips.

"Brady. You shouldn't move; you'll hurt yourself. Please," she whimpered as Gavin drove into her ass.

"I love you, babe. And I'm fine. This little bit of movement is not going to hurt a thing. I might need more than one round."

She panted, "Whatever you need. I love you. I love you both so much."

Gavin nipped her earlobe, his breathing heavy. "Love you too. Fuck, I love your ass, baby. I love fucking you with Brady and watching you come."

Pleasure swelled like a tide pulling back as it turned into a tsunami and barreled for the shoreline. Their grunts and groans combined with the slap of flesh filled the room. They were all Hannah could see and feel.

Her climax crashed into her system. Her hips bucked.

"Oh god!" she wailed.

"Hannah," Gavin bellowed, his dick sliding deep. Brady, let out a deep, long moan and his cock jerked as he thrust.

They thrust over and over again, drawing their pleasure out until they were each utterly spent. Gavin was the first to withdraw. He plopped down onto the bed beside them. She lowered her mouth and brushed it over Brady's. "See, told you that you wouldn't need to do much more than lie there."

Brady grinned. "I bow to the master and am yours to command for the foreseeable future."

"That's all I want. Well, that and you both for the rest of my life. Maybe a couple of kids thrown in."

"Kids, you say?" Brady glanced at Gavin. "Think our girl would look good pregnant, don't you?"

"Yeah, I do. How many you want?" Gavin asked with a teasing glint.

"I was thinking two to start. One with each of you. And then if we decide to get really crazy, after that we can do a coin toss for who gets to father the third kid."

Gavin looked at her, then at Brady, and then back at her. "You want to give me a child, have my baby too?"

Hannah's gaze cut to him and the uncertainty still present in his eyes, like he was afraid it would all vanish into thin air. They would work on that, together. She would reaffirm her feelings for him—for them—as long as it took, until there were no longer any doubts. "Well of course, silly. I love you both. I told you, I'm all in. And that means we're all in this together."

Gavin smiled, his eyes suspiciously wet and shiny. "My own little Christmas miracle."

She felt Brady's shaft begin to harden once more inside her. She gasped. "Again?"

Brady cast her a simmering smirk and said, "Well, all this talk about making kids got me thinking about all the fun we're going to have right here in our bed. We could begin now, if you like."

"Really?" She looked between her men, her heart overflowing with love for them, and the hope for their future filling her with warmth.

"Yeah. I'm hoping you don't want a long engagement," Brady said, lifting her up off his shaft for a moment to rid himself of the condom before guiding his shaft back inside. She bit her bottom lip to contain her soft moan. Brady without a condom, being skin to skin, was better than anything she had ever felt before. And once she was pregnant, they could forgo condoms completely.

"And Brady should be the first. I'll keep wearing a condom until the next kid round," Gavin said, exchanging a meaningful glance with Brady—like they were both in agreement that Brady would go first, be the first to father a child with her.

"Let's hope the first one's a girl to even out some of the testosterone in this house," she murmured before kissing them both: her men, her loves, her world.

This Christmas, she'd given her heart away and been granted so much love in return. Love that she would cherish and hold dear for all the days of their lives. For a woman who had once been tossed away and unloved, it was more than she ever dreamed she might one day have, and she didn't plan on wasting a moment.

In their arms and with their love, anything was possible.

~The End~

His Unexpected Love

CUFFS & SPURS, BOOK TWO

Published by Blushing Books
An Imprint of
ABCD Graphics and Design, Inc.
A Virginia Corporation
977 Seminole Trail #233
Charlottesville, VA 22901

Anya Summers
His Unexpected Love

EBook ISBN: 978-1-947132-12-2
V1
Cover Art by ABCD Graphics & Design
This book contains fantasy themes appropriate for mature readers only. Nothing in this book should be interpreted as Blushing Books' or the author's advocating any non-consensual sexual activity.

Chapter 1

Carter was dog-ass tired and already regretting this unnecessary trip.

If the members of his club, Cuffs and Spurs, in Jackson Hole, Wyoming, hadn't insisted and voted that he, as the owner and founder of their group, personally check out the newest hotspot for those in the lifestyle, he wouldn't be here on a catamaran in the Caribbean. Carter had a myriad number of duties back home on his ranch, the Double J. Instead of training the latest crop of quarter horses this week, he was on board the sleek ocean vessel *Goddess of the Sea*. Carter had to admit the endless blue waves and island that rose up out of the early morning sunlight, spearing the heavens with its lone mountain were beautiful. Not as awe inspiring as the Grand Tetons outside his back door, but it definitely was a sight to behold.

He knew Jared McTavish by reputation only. From what he'd gathered, Jared was a respected Master in the community. It was Tyler Jenson who'd put him and Jared in contact with each other. Carter and Ty went way back, even though they belonged to different clubs.

The only reason Carter was here in the first place was because breeding season for this year on his ranch was over. His two stallions, King Tut and Odin, had each covered a dozen females, starting this past April and ending a week ago. Had the season not already ended, they would have had to dynamite Carter off his ranch.

Typically, the only time he left his ranch was to head into town for supplies or to spend an evening in the club. Otherwise he was at home, working nearly round the clock. He had hired help for both the ranch and the running of the house. But the workload was still nonstop. And this summer had been busier than the last. While he was thankful his business was doing so well, he rarely had time to kick back and relax. And normally, when he did, he was reminded of all that he had to accomplish once his downtime came to a close. The only time he didn't think about work was when he was buried balls-deep in a sub. Fucking got him out of his mind and into the present.

And Carter hadn't been having much of that lately.

There were plenty of subs at his club in Jackson Hole whom he could scene with if he wanted to. But considering he'd had most of them once or twice already and knew which ones wanted a ring on their finger, which ones were nymphos and would fuck anything, and which ones were commitment phobic, they were all getting to be a drag.

He'd even started going outside the sub pool and picking up a tourist or two to get his jollies. But most of them were so straight-laced in the bedroom, they tended to go ape shit if he so much as put his thumb in their ass.

Carter was a lot of things; vanilla wasn't one of them.

When the ferry docked, all Carter could think about was a shower, food, and then bed. Preferably not alone. Handing the bellhop his luggage and carry-on bag, he sauntered off the boat. The gangway plank was a precarious fit for a man his size.

Carter was in shape, always had been, but he was a large man. He knew that. Anyone who saw him knew that—at six foot six, he was a bit hard to miss.

As he rounded the corner off the walkway, a blonde bullet bounced into him and would have tumbled off the dock had he not caught her by the arms. And son of a bitch but she was a looker. Miles of golden blonde hair swung from a high ponytail. She also had cornflower blue eyes that reminded him of the Wyoming sky at midday, and a petite—albeit well-endowed —frame.

"Hey, watch where the hell you're going, damn sasquatch!" she snarled through top-heavy, rose-tinted lips that he'd love to see around his cock.

Carter narrowed his gaze and, instead of cowing or being polite, decided to show this mouthy little princess who was boss. He crowded her body, giving her as stern a glance as he could muster, and said, "Careful. Or someone might take offense to how you speak to them."

She pursed her lips and tossed her hair back. Her gaze lifted and met his with a frank directness that lanced through him. Although, instead of shoving him away as he had assumed she would, the little sub licked her lips—like she wanted to latch those pretty lips of hers onto his body—then leaned her knockout form against him.

Christ. Her pillowy tits smooshed up against his chest, sending all the blood in his head directly to his dick. Thunderbolts of desire rocketed through him when she traced her fine-boned hands over his chest and headed south. Just how far did the sub plan to take her little show?

Fuck, he prayed it was all the way. The muscles in his torso clenched as the tips of her fingers caressed him through the fabric of his tee shirt. He wanted to nudge her hands lower, toward his belt buckle and the part of himself straining against the fabric of his jeans. Carter was all in for whatever this little wanton could lob his way, and so was his cock. Pleasure Island had become infinitely more interesting than it was previously.

"Oh, I'm sorry, Sir. I thought you would have noticed a little thing like me," she murmured, saccharine sweet with a seductive expression on her gorgeous face that would likely lead men to their doom.

A little too sweet. That should have been the tipoff. But all his brain power was currently located in his crotch.

"You can always make it up to me, darlin," he said, already envisioning his cock in her mouth—among other places—with her baby blue gaze looking up at him adoringly.

Her smile grew brighter and she raised a single golden brow as he bent his head down. Would she let him taste her succulent, bow-shaped mouth? Then her delicate hands still splayed against his chest, which had seemed so inviting a moment ago, shoved against him with such Teutonic force that she knocked him off his feet. She muttered, "Cool off, big guy. I don't have time for your Dom bullshit."

Shock riddled his form as he tumbled through the air. And then his body hit water.

The mildly warm water jarred his body as he plunged beneath the surface. The lust she had ignited transformed into fury. He hadn't flown thousands of miles to get dunked into the ocean by an uppity sub. He surfaced, sputtering sea water from his mouth. Luckily, he'd always been athletically inclined, but swimming in his favorite boots wasn't easy. However a lesser man would have drowned. Damn things were likely ruined by the unexpected dunking.

Fuck.

Carter swam to a nearby ladder attached to the docks and hauled himself up out of the water. He reached the top rung just in time to watch that little sub's gorgeous ass sashay away. A large male hand helped him up over the top until he stood, sopping wet and ready to roar.

Carter shouted, "What the fuck kind of greeting was that? Who the hell was she?"

Because he wasn't done with that sub in the slightest. That gorgeous ass of hers was just begging for a strong hand to show her who was boss. Preferably *his* hand, with her ass bare and glowing ruby red from his touch. And then he intended to leave the island because he hadn't traveled all this way for a headache of this magnitude. Carter had his own problems and didn't need anyone else's.

The man who'd helped him back onto the dock was dressed in black slacks and a long sleeved blue dress shirt. His ginger hair was longer than the average businessman's, and his eyes were hidden behind a pair of aviators. How he could wear formal business wear in this heat and humidity was beyond Carter.

"Carter. I'm Jared McTavish. I apologize that your welcome was a bit wetter than intended," he said in a rolling Scottish brogue.

"Yeah, well, you can charter me the first boat off the fucking island after I discipline that sub. I didn't come here for this. I have a herd of horses to train. What kind of establishment are you running anyhow if a submissive can act out like that?" Carter demanded, his voice booming as he yelled at the man.

Jared nodded. "I understand your concern. Jenna will be dealt with at the club tonight by my hand. I can promise you that."

"Do all the subs run roughshod over the place?" Carter asked. If so, then he was gone. That was something he ensured at his club: that submissives knew their place and how to act. When one stepped a toe out of line, she was disciplined and dealt with accordingly.

Jared shook his head and said, a grimace on his face, "No.

And I admit, I've never had one do something precisely like that. I can promise you, I will rectify the matter and see to her discipline. At least stay the night, see if I can change your mind. If not, I will have a ferry ready for you first thing tomorrow, or could even charter one of the DFC's jets to fly you home." He gestured toward a waiting golf cart. "If you would like to come with me, I will escort you to your villa. Additionally, I will have your clothes dry cleaned—on the house, of course. If there's anything that is a total loss, it will be replaced at no cost to you."

"And that sub?" Carter said. It was clear Jared wasn't remiss in his duties as a Master, but he still wasn't sold on the place.

"Will be dealt with, I can promise you that," Jared responded, his face unreadable behind his aviators.

"I want her for my week-long stay. Clearly you have some subs who need to be properly trained," Carter replied, certain he had lost his mind the moment that little thing had pressed herself against him. A saner man would walk away and find greener pastures.

Jared grimaced. "We pride ourselves on safe, sane, and consensual."

Carter snorted. "Relax. I won't hurt her. I might tan her fucking hide a few times, but I would never truly harm a sub. If that's what you think of me—"

"I mean no offense, but I protect those under my care, including my employees," Jared replied, his countenance and bearing staunchly protective. Like he would be only too happy to put Carter on the nearest boat if there was even a hint of the possibility a submissive would be harmed by him.

Carter respected the hell out of that. They did the same with any of the subs who came into their club. Fuck, he might actually like Jared, if he hadn't had such a rude and wet welcome.

"I'll stay. But I want her or I walk," Carter tossed out the ultimatum, again wondering if it was a wise move on his part.

"Understood. I will see what I can do to arrange that Jenna is your submissive this week." Jared said, "If you'll follow me, we can get you situated. I've procured one of our exclusive luxury villas for your stay."

Carter nodded, trailing behind him to the cart. He had a name for his little termagant. Jenna. It suited her.

Chapter 2

She shouldn't have done what she did.

Jenna knew her actions had consequences. They always did. Maybe if she wasn't so tired from working late last night at the Dungeon Club serving drinks, and then being up at the ass-crack of dawn to run errands for the front desk, just to earn a little extra cash, then perhaps she wouldn't have sassed the man—among other things, like shoving him into the ocean.

Way to go and completely screw up the job she needed. Jenna was just so damn tired. The burdens she carried got heavier by the day.

Jenna hadn't meant to run into that guest. She'd had her head down, trying to flash forward through her day, and hadn't seen him until she'd plowed into his firm, broad chest. The rebound almost knocked her off her feet. His hands had closed around her biceps and short circuited her brain patterns... because, heaven help her, what a man. A dominant alpha with dark chestnut hair that nearly grazed his massive shoulders. His forthright hazel gaze had been brown, with specks of green and gold. Full lips that were shrouded by a few days' growth of dark stubble. Sinful didn't even begin to cover his handsome face. She hadn't been kidding when she'd called him sasquatch. The man was a freaking giant. So large he'd blocked out the sun—with a little help from his black Stetson.

Her body had purred at his innocent touch. And it had fueled the flames of her anger, much like poking an angry bear. Before her brain had time to process what she was doing, she was shoving him into the water.

But that was why she now stood, somewhat contrite, before her boss, Jared McTavish. Master and owner of this fine island establishment. From the way his gaze assessed her from behind his desk, Jenna knew she was walking a razor-fine line.

Dammit.

"Jenna, I can't begin to understand why you would act out that way with a guest. Carter Jones is the owner of a lifestyle club in Wyoming and someone I'm hoping the island can do business with. Mind telling me what happened today? And why you took it upon yourself to so rudely welcome a guest?" Jared asked, sitting behind his desk, decked out in club gear. The Dom was a beautiful man, with his expanse of muscular chest bare.

There was no excuse she could offer, at least not one he would understand. She hid her trembling fingers. "No, Sir."

She couldn't really explain it herself. Except that man with his *I'm a big bad Dom* attitude and forthright gaze had pushed her buttons the wrong way. The fact that he apparently believed that because she was submissive he could swagger off the boat, wave his dick her way, and she should be thankful for it, had pushed all of her buttons—all the wrong ones. Her mom had always said she must have a recessive redhead gene, because she could go off with the right provocation and there was no coming back once her fury had been launched.

Carter's attitude was archaic and had made her see red. Before her brain had really connected with her higher reasoning skills, she'd shoved the man into the bay. In her opinion, the Dom deserved it. That didn't mean she was willing to risk her job, the job she needed desperately.

"Well, I can't let it go unpunished. If you want to continue working here, you will be publicly disciplined in the club. Do you understand?" Jared asked, his gaze clear and unyielding.

She winced. It was her fault. The punishment was one of her own making that she couldn't see a way around. Jenna would pay the piper. That was all she seemed to do. Work. Then rob Peter to pay Paul—or, in this case, her father's medical bills and sister's tuition. There were days when her life was just one big ball of crud. Days when she felt like life had chewed her up and spit her out.

Exhaustion was a normal state of being for Jenna. She was the one who held everything together for her family. If she screwed up, they paid the price. Just once she'd like to lean back and know that her world wouldn't come tumbling down while she rested.

"I understand. And I am sorry. I was tired and in a hurry and he…" What? Had awed her with his sheer size? Had ignited a slow burn in her body at feeling his hard, masculine body against hers? Had turned her insides into putty at the unwavering dominance in his stance? That there had been a part of Jenna that had desperately wanted to sink into him. Right there on the docks and forget everything else, all her responsibilities and the people counting on her. Let his big body not only block out the sun but the rest of the world too.

It had been her guilt more than anything that had kick started her fury. Guilt over her wish to relinquish her duties, even for a moment.

Pathetic: table for one.

"Did he do something, Jenna? If he so much as crooked a finger at you without your permission, say the word and this ends now. I will have him escorted off the island if he manhandled you in any way," Jared asked.

He would do it too. She could see it in his fervent gaze. Jared was one of the good ones, protecting her and the rest of the submissives on the island the way he did. Not that he wasn't an exacting taskmaster, because he totally was. Yet he would put a potential partnership on the line for her if harm had come to her. There weren't many men—let alone many employers—who would see to their employee's welfare above that of the company. As much as that warmed her, and as much as she'd love to toss Carter under the bus, Jenna couldn't allow Jared to lose business because of her own stupidity. It had been her issues that had initiated her internal combustion to nuclear meltdown levels.

"No, Master J. It was my fault. And I submit myself to whatever punishment you deem necessary," she said, straightening her shoulders. She owned up to her part in this. Would the cowboy?

"Thank you for being honest. Strip and put these on. You will be publicly flogged in the club," Jared commanded, putting a black pair of cuffs on his desk.

"Yes, Sir," she replied, her voice barely above a whisper.

Ignoring the fear and embarrassment at having to disrobe before her boss, Jenna undressed. She just prayed he didn't want sex from her. If there was one thing she never mixed, it was who she slept with and her work. It was too important that she be able to earn a living. No man, no Dom was worth losing a job over. From what she'd heard about Jared, he didn't sleep with the help, but she'd had bosses before attempt to use sex as a weapon.

Jenna folded her waitress uniform up and stacked it on the nearby leather chair. Then she slid the cuffs on around her wrists, fastening the buckles. She wasn't a prude by any means, but still she was uncomfortable. Jared rose from his seat and approached, looking every inch a Dom in his leather pants and shit-kicker boots. Her breath caught in her throat when she spied what he was holding. In his large palms was a black leather collar with silver chains attached to it.

"Bend your head forward," he ordered, his face a stern mask.

Unwilling to spark his anger and chance risking her job, Jenna did as he asked. He affixed the collar around her throat. For her, it was akin to wearing a scarlet letter. Wearing a collar just for punishment, from someone who wasn't her own Dom or Master, added to the humiliation—and besides, she preferred cuffs as a symbol of ownership.

Then Jared connected her wrist cuffs to a short length of chain that imprisoned her hands together before her. He slid a black leather flogger into his back pocket, then, with his hand around the second length of chain that acted much in the same manner as a dog leash, led her out of his office.

On the elevator, he gave her further instructions. "Once we are in the club, you are not to speak unless it is to use your safeword. Remind me again what it is?"

"Red, Sir."

"Good. Easy to remember. Deep breaths, lass, this part will be over shortly," he murmured, chucking her chin gently with his free hand.

This part? What did he mean by *this part*? Before she could ask him, the elevator doors slid open with a quiet ding onto the club level. All other thoughts fled as Jenna ignored the interested stares of club goers and focused all her energy on Jared's back. He stalked ahead of her, his long legs eating up the distance to the raised dais in the center of the club, and she had to hurry to keep up with him. In the center of the stage was a leather padded sawhorse. Shame inflamed her cheeks at needing to be disciplined before the whole club.

She kept her lips tightly closed as Jared attached her wrists to the sawhorse. Jenna was bent forward, the horse turned into a stockade. The way he positioned her body, her naked rump was presented to everyone in the club. Then he spread her legs apart and fastened Velcro cuffs around her ankles. So now every club attendee had a direct view of her pussy.

Lovely. Her day just kept on getting worse by the minute.

Anticipation tingled along her spine as Jared moved around behind her. An unmistakable figure emerged from the shadows. His hard gaze was trained on hers with a satisfied gleam in their dark depths. She didn't bat an eye or lower her gaze but stared at Carter head on.

"Jenna, I'm going to begin. If it gets to be too much, use your safeword, lass," Jared ordered quietly in her ear.

She nodded. The flogger cracked against her bum. The leather straps snapped and cracked against her skin. Jenna cried out at the unexpected force of the blow.

Then Jared swatted her three more times in rapid succession. Jenna's gaze was unwavering as she glared defiantly at Carter. With every stroke, her blood heated. The air whooshed from her lungs. Her cry was a garbled, high-pitched moan. The more blows Jared struck against her ass cheeks, the louder her wails became. They were a mixture of pronounced pleasure and pain.

And through it all, she stared at Carter. Not cowing or bowing to his dominant air, but daring him, defying him with every harsh lash against her ass. She'd earned this discipline, yet she would never yield to the likes of a Dom like Carter, who apparently thought the world should bend to his will. It was there in his bearing as he glowered at her.

Except her body was enjoying their wordless glaring contest. A little too much. Jenna imagined it was Carter issuing her discipline. His rather large hands holding the flogger and raining brutal swats to her behind and making it burn. Flames licked at her core and sparked her arousal.

Through the pain, she held on, not willing to give Carter an inch as he viewed her discipline. The rest of the patrons hardly existed. For Jenna, the only ones present were her and Carter. It infuriated her that this man had such a hold on her.

The flogging reached a crescendo. The fever pitch of Jared's whacks to her bum made her eyes water, and heaven help her but her body overrode her unwillingness to show weakness before the enemy.

She came. Hard.

Jenna screamed. "Ahhh."

Her body shook from the sheer force of her climax. She strained against her bonds as tremors racked her frame. But she never, for one second, took her eyes off Carter. The man didn't blink, his face unreadable. His jaw was clenched, his mouth a firm, unyielding line.

Then Jared put a warm blanket around her shoulders as he gently began undoing her restraints. Once her body was free from the sawhorse, Jared more firmly wrapped her form up in the blanket, hefted her in his strong arms, and carted her to a nearby couch.

Her boss sat with her cradled against his chest. But she didn't feel arousal with him, just comfort. Jared stroked a gentle hand down her blanket-covered back. "You did well. But that was only the first half of your punishment."

"What do you mean, Sir? I thought you said…" Then in her haze she remembered he'd mentioned something about 'this part'.

"That your punishment was to be of my choosing. There was more than one Dom you harmed with your actions today," Jared responded, his gaze warm but firm in his resolve.

"I don't understand," she replied, but oh, she did. The pit of her stomach sank into her toes. He meant Carter. The man who'd driven her to temporary insanity.

"The rest of your punishment will be to serve Master Carter for the next week. Do you understand, Jenna? It means you will belong to him this week as his submissive," Jared explained, the command behind his words firm and not a little daunting.

All the air in the room vanished. Jenna had to beat back the fear clawing at her chest to keep herself from hyperventilating. She had to submit to that Dom? Carter was the offended Dom, but these were Jared's rules. He decided on punishment for the subs in his employ, and had chosen to hand her off to the sasquatch. Jenna didn't have a choice, at least not any good ones. If she wanted to remain employed here on the island, her only option was to do as Master J directed and submit to Carter this week. She cursed at herself internally at feeling the wetness trailing over her cheeks. She hated showing weakness of any kind.

There was only one course, one road which she could tread. Jenna needed her paycheck too damn much to be able to refuse. There was no other way around the punishment, as barbaric as it might be. There were too many people depending upon her and the money she made here on the island for her to welch now.

She saw no way out of her predicament. Sensing the behemoth's presence nearby, she nodded her acquiescence and responded to Jared, "Yes, Sir."

"Carter, you will let me know if there are any problems with her discipline," Jared addressed the damn sasquatch over her shoulder.

Unable to stand the suspense, Jenna confronted her punishment head on. The Dom was a six foot six—give or take an inch —cowboy who opted for jeans instead of leather pants, and a black Stetson. And the way his gaze traveled over her, the possession and unbridled lust he showed her in his dark gaze, caused her internal emergency sensors to blare code red.

From a mere glance, she understood the man would attempt to flay her open, both heart and soul, and enjoy the unmaking. He'd turn her into a slave, try to bend her to his will, and she only prayed that she was strong enough to withstand his dominance. There was too much riding on her shoulders to fail.

"That I will. Come on now, darlin', let's go get ourselves acquainted," Carter said, the deep timbre of his voice making her think of drinking hundred proof whiskey around a campfire. Backed into a corner, she accepted the proffered hand. His work roughened fingers closed around hers, and a torrent of tingles erupted in her system where he touched her. Carter helped her off Jared's lap. Her free hand clutched at the blanket around her shoulders. Jenna infused her gaze with every ounce of her wrath at having her choice taken from her and directed it at the man of the hour.

The sasquatch had the audacity to return her glare with a sardonic grin. Tremors raced along her spine.

The disparity and difference in height as he dwarfed her left her feeling unsettled. The man reminded her of a mountain: strong and immovable. With a victorious smirk on his lips that she wanted to remove. Carter swooped her up into his arms when she wobbled on her feet as her resolve to see her punishment through wavered. He carted her, blanket and all. He didn't take her to a nearby couch or scene area, but headed past curious onlookers and patrons directly out of the club.

Jenna fought the distinct and altogether surprising urge to turn in to him as his musky scent, which was part dark woodsy spice and part manly Carter, enveloped her. It made her want to rub her face against his chest and see if his skin tasted as good as he smelled.

Dammit.

She couldn't deny that she was attracted to him. As much as she wanted to beat the arrogant man upside the head with her serving tray, his touch, his arms around her, rekindled her internal forge, and by the time he placed her in the front passenger seat of his cart, she was thoroughly aroused. Watching him saunter around to the driver's side and slide in beside her, Jenna understood she was going to have one hell of a difficult time submitting to Carter while remaining unmoved by him.

She clutched at the blanket around her shoulders. Looking out at the illuminated path, she tried to center herself, her posture rigid in the seat.

"Relax. I'm not an ogre," Carter said, his deep baritone

causing her chest to buzz with tingly sensations. He drove the cart with precision and command over the path, but she could feel his gaze on her. He kept studying her with his enigmatic gaze.

"I never said you were, Sir," she murmured. His presence was all-consuming, dominating the small space of the cart, and she hated that he stirred her.

"If you truly object to being with me, I won't force you," he commented as he parked the cart beneath his villa and shifted all his focus toward her.

It was more of a concession than she'd believed she would receive from him. She couldn't deny her attraction any more than she needed air to breathe. It didn't mean she was okay with Jared forcing her hand. She consented to being with Carter but she had reservations about it. Loads of them. She admitted, "I don't object to it, much. But forgive me, Sir, I'm not sure why you would want me after this morning."

"What can I say? I enjoy a challenge. Besides, I'm used to working with finicky mares on my ranch and get a thrill at having such untamed beauty bend to my hand and my will," Carter murmured, his voice gruff and low.

Jenna curled her fingers into her palms against the blanket to keep from wrapping them around his throat and strangling him. The damn sasquatch had compared her to a horse. She was not a freaking horse but a grown woman. She might be submissive, but she would fight him tooth and nail this week. He might have control of her body, but she would never grant him anything more, and certainly not her full submission.

She'd be lucky if she didn't murder him by week's end.

Chapter 3

Carter almost laughed at the steam emitting from Jenna's ears over his remarks. She was a firecracker and definitely spurred his interest. Never before had he had a submissive with such passion. The challenge she presented, captivated him.

Then there was the little fact that after seeing her waltz into the club, her killer body on display, he could have practically cut diamonds with his cock he'd been so hard. She had perfect, round, high breasts, with deep rose nipples that had been puckered into hard points. Her torso was sleek, he could span her waist with both of his hands, and then her hips curved out, becomingly framing her bare pussy. He could imagine her long, lithe legs wrapped around his waist as he fucked her senseless.

Not to mention that she'd held his gaze as Jared had flogged her. Passion had suffused her expression, her mouth open. The high-pitched moans she'd emitted had fueled his lust. Carter, for once, was glad he'd been enchanted by her face and watching her orgasm. If he'd slipped around and viewed the scene from the other direction, watching Jared redden her behind, he didn't know if he would have been able to control himself, and would likely have come in his jeans like an unschooled youth. Or he would already be balls-deep inside her.

As it was, he didn't want a perfunctory screw with the little sub. He wanted all of her. He wanted to make her crave his touch and have her gift him with her submission on a freaking platter.

And he could surmise from the tense set to her shoulders and 'fuck off' attitude that he had his work cut out for him. Never let it be said that he didn't rise to the occasion when it was warranted. And Jenna commanded every ounce of his control.

He helped her from the cart and led her into the villa. The place was luxurious, spacious and airy with its circular design. His favorite part was how intricate and detailed every piece of furniture was, even in the kitchen. There were hidden loops everywhere to attach an unruly submissive's cuffs. It was something he was taking note of: all the little extras he might want to add to his own home when he got a spare minute.

The bed was an extra-large king which was downright perfect for a man his size. Often, when he had to travel for business, he'd end up in a bed where his feet hung over the end. That wouldn't be a problem here. And the thing he enjoyed most was the small dungeon area equipped with one of his favorite devices: a St. Andrew's Cross.

He had plans to strap her in and fuck her until his legs gave out.

"Have a seat on the couch," he ordered.

She shot him a furious glance but then complied. They were going to have to work on that, among other things. He went to the dresser and withdrew his special cuffs, with his club's logo on them and his initials burned into the dark brown saddle colored leather.

He strode back over to the couch and sank down beside her. "Give me your wrists."

She stretched out her hands. It caused the blanket shrouding her small form to slide down and expose a wealth of her creamy skin. He had to draw his tongue back into his head at the sight. She was so gorgeous, she made him ache.

And then he slid one of his cuffs around her wrist. At the feel of her hand trembling against his, shock infused him, followed by the need to comfort her. Of all the things he would have expected from this brash and brave submissive, her fear sliced him open to the bone.

"Jenna, look at me," he murmured, waiting until her cornflower gaze met his. "You have nothing to fear from me. Understand? I realize you don't know me yet, but I won't ever harm you. Will I push your boundaries this week? Yes. Do I plan to make you come, repeatedly, to the point you won't be able to walk the next day? Yes. Will I discipline you should you disobey me? Absolutely. But you don't have to be afraid of me, all right?"

She nodded and blinked back moisture from her gaze. "Yes, Sir. I am sorry about this morning."

"Sorry that you did it or sorry that you're being punished for it?" he asked.

"And if I said the latter?" she asked as he slid the second cuff on, pleased that her trembles had diminished.

"Then I would say thank you for being honest with me," he murmured. The chit was completely incorrigible.

"Forgive me, but are you sure it's me you want this week?"

"One hundred percent, so stop fussing and trying to finagle a way out. You belong to me this week, darlin'."

Her demeanor shifted from somewhat open and friendly, to rabidly incensed. Carter would put a stop to her attitude. Right. Now. Without preamble or warning, he shifted her onto his lap and gripped her chin in his hand.

"Look at me," he ordered. And then he waited for Jenna to comply. It took her a few heartbeats. He noticed the pulse at her throat flutter.

Then she finally, with aching slowness, lifted her gaze,

lingering when she reached his lips before ascending completely. Her pupils were dilated and her breathing shallow. He bit back a grin. She desired him. That was as good a place as any to start.

While one hand cupped her jaw and held her gaze steady on his, his free hand roamed over her body. He palmed one of her apple-sized breasts, and was pleased when he rasped his thumb over the nipple and it puckered into a beaded point.

"Now that I have your attention, we are going to go over my rules and discuss your hard limits. The rules first. In my presence, you will always be nude and wearing my cuffs. You will submit yourself to me wherever, and whenever I choose. I do not put up with mouthy, disobedient subs. If you are glib, talk back, or refuse to do as requested, you will be punished in the manner of my choosing. Understood?" he asked, searching her gaze.

"Total domination and the loss of my free will. Got it, Sir," she said and then bit her lower lip when he pinched her nipple. Her eyes went wide and she uttered a quiet moan. This little sub liked the pain.

He had to contain his chuckle at her response. She would not break easily, his little firebrand. "Pretty much, darlin', may as well get used to it. Now, what are your hard limits?"

"The only thing that is a definite no is medical play. I can't stand needles. I've been known to pass out from the flu shot. And I don't necessarily care for public scenes."

"And yet you submitted to your punishment with Jared. Are you and he an item?"

"Jared? God, no. It's not that he's not attractive—he is—but he's my boss and I have a strict no sleeping with the boss policy," she said with a shake of her head.

"What about the rest of the Doms on the island?" Carter asked. He didn't share. Some Doms enjoyed topping a sub together. He wasn't one of them.

"No, there's no one."

"Why is that? You're a beautiful woman," he said frankly, rather curious about the beauty on his lap.

She shrugged. "Because I work here and that policy deal, I tend to extend to other Doms in the workplace."

"But the guests to the island…"

"None of whom I've wanted. I'm not sure why it matters to you. I'm yours this week," she murmured and dropped her gaze.

"It matters because for me to have your full attention, I need to know that there isn't someone else. I don't poach on another Dom's territory. So have you been with a Dom since you started working here?" he asked.

"No. You will be the first. On the island, I mean. There was a club I attended in Tampa, but it wasn't as well policed as this place and you really had to be careful," she said, regret lacing her voice.

"And were you careful?" he asked as his hand left her breast and stroked over her abdomen down to her thighs.

"I tried to be," she admitted, going stiff in his arms. Hmmm. That was something he would shelve for later, once she trusted him more.

"I see. Well, I can promise you I won't hurt you beyond a good flogging or caning. But you need to be honest with me, darlin', since we don't know each other well yet. If something I do hurts or is uncomfortable, you need to tell me. With that in mind, what's your safeword?"

"Red, Sir," she murmured and then gasped. Her eyes went wide with arousal as his fingers stroked through her nether lips.

Shit. She was wet. For him. Her lips parted, and she mewled in the back of her throat as he circled her clit. Sliding his hand on her chin around to her nape, he slid his hands into her hair, holding her steady, and lowered his mouth over hers.

She tasted like his every wet fantasy brought to startling life. He claimed her lips, nipping and sucking on her top lip before plunging his tongue inside her mouth. Heaven. That's what he found as he slanted his mouth over hers. Her fine-boned hands slid into his hair, knocking his hat off, and gripped him tight. Jenna kissed him back with a voracious need that called forth all his desires.

His cock strained in his jeans. His fingers toyed with her nub, circling and flicking the tiny bud as it swelled for him. Unable to help himself, he stroked through her labia to her pussy entrance. Then he penetrated her and began finger fucking her. She moaned into his mouth but opened her legs wider for his touch. Her pussy gripped his fingers, like scorching hot silk surrounding his digits.

This was what he wanted: Jenna writhing and moaning for his touch. She was seductive in her desire, canting her hips, craving the rigorous plunging of his fingers. Carter didn't tease her or draw her need out. He needed to feel her come at his touch. Especially after watching her discipline. It gave him a heady thrill that no one else on the island had experienced her passion. She rocked her hips, thrusting against his fingers. His dick strained to be released and replace his digits. She mewled into his mouth. As he drank her cries, his tongue mimicked the ardent finger fucking.

Her pussy gripped him, squeezing his fingers. Then her channel spasmed as she came. She quaked in his arms from the force of her climax. He drank her moans, not stopping the motion of his fingers until she melted against him. Only then did he finally break away. She was gorgeous. Her mouth slightly open. Her eyes shut. Her breathing came in short pants. The pulse in her neck fluttered.

She lifted her gaze and pleasure flowed through him. She wanted him. Wanted more. All good places for them to start.

Carter lifted the fingers coated with her essence and sucked them into his mouth. She tasted like a fine Bordeaux, one he had every intention of sampling for hours on end. "Mmm, your pussy tastes mighty fine. All right, darlin', that was a real nice introduction. But I'm going to put you up on the cross and test your boundaries a bit."

"But what about you, Sir? You didn't get to come," she murmured, her blue gaze forthright, and while she'd just climaxed, there was hunger in her depths. His gut clenched, desire lancing through him. The thought of just having her ride him right then and there flashed through his mind. Yet he wanted more from her than a simple perfunctory release. Although… perhaps he should just get the first time with her out of the way so he could focus and regain his control.

"There'll be plenty of time for that. Why, is there something you want?" he asked, curious about what she would do.

She hesitated, and her gaze dropped to his mouth and then to his torso before she nodded. His breath lodged in his chest as he waited for her to make the next move. Would she be so bold?

"Yes. I want you… this," she placed a delicate hand against his erection straining against his jeans, "I want to taste you."

Jenna lifted her gaze and blasted him with lust. Who the hell was he to argue with that? Her hand against his dick felt like a brand. At the moment, there was nothing he wanted more than to watch her pink lips close over his cock and suck him dry.

"And so you shall. I'm all yours," he murmured. His blood pumped in his ears, waiting to see what she would do. His body was electrified with need.

With his permission, she nodded and shifted until she knelt before him on the floor between his legs. She made a picture, naked on her knees before him, wearing his cuffs, with passion clouding her visage. Then her hands were at the waistband of his jeans. She unlatched his belt. Her delicate fingers brushed the muscles of his abdomen and he couldn't stop the shiver that erupted.

Fuck, she was making him act like a teenager with his first woman. His stalwart, legendary control deserted him at her touch.

Then she unclasped the button of his jeans and drew the zipper down. Her hand slid beneath the elastic band of his gray boxer briefs and freed his turgid cock.

He groaned at the feel of her small hands wrapped around his shaft. Pleasure pooled in his loins. Jenna stared at his cock, licked her pink lips, and then leaned forward. Her pink tongue darted out and laved the head, catching the drop of pre-cum glimmering on the crest. At the first caress of her tongue against his flesh, his gut quivered and Carter dug his hands into the sofa. She swirled her tongue around the head with teasing licks. He felt every brush lance through him. With one hand gripped around his shaft base, she lowered her mouth over his crown and enveloped his cock in her wet heat.

Fuck, she had a sweet mouth. She watched him, her baby blues trained on him as she worked her mouth up and down his length. She didn't hold back, and her gaze grew heavy-lidded as she sucked his dick, squeezing the hilt with one hand while the other massaged his sac. She enveloped his full length, until he could feel the back of her throat, and then sucked him until he thought his eyes were going to roll back inside his head permanently.

He gave her as much freedom as possible, granting Jenna free rein while she gave him head until he could no longer restrain his control. Carter gripped the sides of her head and pumped his dick inside her hot fucking mouth. She moaned around him, her hands sliding to his ass as she opened her mouth further, and hollowing her cheeks as she took him inside. Her fingers dug into his ass.

His balls drew taut and his cock swelled. Carter couldn't hold back as pleasure electrified along his spine. Unleashing his inner beast, he fucked her mouth, pummeling it with his shaft. And her slight mewls of enjoyment drove him out of his mind. His hands tightened on her head. His hips pounded. It began at the base of his spine and his balls. His dick jerked and he exploded.

"Aw fuck, that it's, darlin. Fuck yeah!" he bellowed. Hot streams of cum filled her mouth as he climaxed. Tidal waves of ecstasy scored his system and he trembled. Jenna worked her throat, swallowing his semen. She continued to lap at his dick like it was a tasty treat.

She controlled her movements, accepting every drop of cum until he was empty. Then she lifted her mouth. As she released his semi-hard shaft slowly, her eyes never left his. Fuck, he'd known she was full of fire, but she'd blown more than his cock—his mind as well.

He hauled her back onto his lap and kissed her. He could taste himself on her tongue and it drove him wild. Carter kissed her until she was pliant and whimpering in his arms. He kissed her until he felt his cock re-engage for another round. And then he stood, never breaking contact with her lips, and carried her over to the cross.

Getting dunked into the ocean, as far as he was concerned, was the best fucking thing ever to have happened to him.

JENNA MOANED into Carter's mouth. Her fingers threaded into his hair as he carried her as if she weighed nothing. She was so aroused after giving him head. She wanted him. Who was she kidding? She'd wanted him the moment she'd run into him on the docks. That had been part of her problem. And partially why she'd reacted the way she had when he had acted like he was the master of the universe.

But my god, the man was huge—everywhere. A good, solid eight inches in length, and so wide her middle finger and thumb didn't meet circling him. Her sasquatch nickname was more than appropriate.

Then he set her on her feet next to the St. Andrew's Cross. She whimpered at the loss of his arms around her and his warmth. Carter, his hand firm but gentle, fastened her body onto the cross. First he attached her wrist cuffs—his cuffs—spreading her arms in a wide V above her head. Then he was fastening her ankles into leather cuffs, the position spreading her legs wide so that she resembled a starfish. Carter attached a leather strap across her waist.

Once she was completely locked down, he kissed her; a hot, drugging tangle of tongues and lips that left her whimpering for more. Carter lifted his head and winked. Then he hastened to the nearby armoire. His back was to her, and her gaze caressed the muscled, sinewy lines. Carter removed his boots, then shucked his jeans and boxer briefs in a single, economical move. The sight of him from behind, from his back to his well-formed butt, to his powerfully muscled thighs and calves, made her mouth water. She marveled as his muscles moved and rippled while he opened drawers and withdrew items for the upcoming session, setting those things on a nearby table. It barely registered what he withdrew from the armoire. Her eyes were on Carter.

Then he swiveled back towards her in his full naked glory.

She moaned deep in her chest.

The man quite simply took her breath away. He was six and a half feet of power-packed muscles. His shoulders were so broad they barely fit through a doorframe, and ropey muscle lined them. His arms were thick and with every move his muscles bunched and flowed, displaying the power within them. His chest was covered with dark fur. Not a thick pelt reminiscent of a sasquatch, but enough to cover his perfectly formed pectorals and make her purr.

His chest hair tapered down into a single dark happy trail that descended down over his corded, defined abs. The happy trail ended at his most impressive manhood. He'd tasted smoky and salty on her tongue. The skin of his cock was satiny smooth, and he was so large he'd stretched her mouth to painful proportions. She licked her lips, wanting to taste him again, feel his girth in her mouth.

His thighs were thickly muscled and powerful as he approached her. His erection saluted her as he neared.

Carter gave her a seductive grin. Then he leaned forward and sucked one of her nipples into his mouth. He curled his tongue around the bud, teasing her. Then he affixed a small cylindrical tube over her nipple, twisted the lever on top, and it suctioned her nipple to a near aching extent. At her whimper, he shot her a wicked, knowing grin and shifted to her other breast before doing the same with its twin.

The way the nipple suckers added just the right amount of pressure on the buds sent torrents of need coursing through her body. Then Carter gave each of them one more twist. The increase in pressure spliced the pleasure with pain. Her mouth fell open on a moan.

And then the big behemoth shocked her by kneeling before her. Raised up like she was on the cross with her legs wide open, it put his face near her crotch.

"Now, no coming, darlin', until I allow it." Carter's smile was wolfish. He kept his gaze trained on hers as he swiped through her folds with his tongue.

He explored her pussy with his tongue, testing her and locating her hotspots, sliding his tongue beneath her hood. Teasing her clit with languorous flicks that were driving her out of her ever-loving mind. He nibbled on her puffy, swollen labia folds and teased her pussy with penetration only to parry and withdraw until she was a writhing, seething mass of need.

It wasn't until he had mapped out her pussy that the man went for the freaking gold. She strained, craving more friction as he fucked her with his tongue. Jenna whimpered and mewled. And through it all, he kept his gaze on her as he feasted on her pussy. She was aching, needing release in the worst way.

"Please, Sir, please let me come," she pleaded, and hated that she was begging. But holy mother mercy, the man had a wicked tongue and should be crowned the king of oral. She'd never in her life been eaten out so thoroughly.

"Not just yet. You're doing beautifully, Jenna. Give me more, surrender, and I will let you come, I swear. Put yourself into my hands," Carter murmured and then resumed eating her pussy with such relish, she struggled to maintain her control.

She didn't want to give him everything. But with every stroke of his tongue as it lapped against her folds and swiped over her clit, she hung over the edge. A simple push would launch her over it.

And then Carter, damn him, penetrated her with two digits, thrusting his fingers inside her quivering sheath while he sucked on her swollen clit. He pumped his fingers, adding a third digit. As he withdrew them, he curled them forward so he was rubbing her G-spot. The wave of pleasure grew to maddening heights and enveloped her until she willingly flung herself over the cliff.

Her body turned fluid under his hands and mouth. Her nipples throbbed in agonized pleasure.

"Come," Carter growled against her clit and bit down, just as his fingers thrust inside.

Jenna burst and flooded his hand as she came. Hard. Fast. It stole the air from her lungs. Her mouth hung open as her pussy quaked and her body shuddered. Her nipples throbbed in the suckers. Her head hung low, her gaze half-lidded as Carter withdrew his fingers from her pussy. He sucked them into his mouth and lapped up all her dew for a second time that night.

It was the sexiest thing she'd witnessed in forever: this big huge man enjoying her flavor like she was a delicacy. Carter rose to his full height. He removed the nipple suckers and it set off a series of flutters in her pussy. He walked to the table and returned, rolling a condom down his thick length.

Then he stood before her, his cock in his hand, and rubbed

the tip through her drenched folds. She moaned in the back of her throat.

Carter lined his cock up at her opening and ordered, "Look at me."

She hadn't realized she'd shut her eyes. She lifted her heavy lids. His face was awash with hunger. And then he rolled his hips and thrust. Her mouth fell open as he furrowed deep inside her.

He was so big, stretching her tissues to almost painful lengths. He gritted his teeth as he thrust, working his girth inside until his balls smooshed against her rear. He kept his gaze trained on her as he pounded. His cock slid over every single one of her nerve endings—and some she didn't realize she had.

He hammered his shaft, the sound of flesh slapping against flesh filling the villa. Her moans grew louder as he thrust, and he was all she could see. She wanted it to last but she could feel the blurry edges of her climax near.

"Carter, Sir, please. Oh god," she moaned.

"Go on over, darlin', come for me," he ordered, groaning as he jackhammered his cock inside her, unleashing his control, his fingers digging into her hips so hard they would likely leave bruises. His moans mingled with hers as he fucked her.

Her climax detonated in her system. Her pussy spasmed around his plunging cock and she screamed, "Carter."

Waves of ecstasy bombarded her as she came. Dimly she heard Carter roar as he strained. His shaft surged inside her clenching sheath and she came again, fluttering around his member as his cum filled his condom.

Jenna sagged as she felt her body begin to shut down from all the orgasms and the strain of her discipline that night. Dimly she felt Carter withdraw his shaft from her body. There was movement around her but she struggled to keep her eyes open. Her ankles were released from their restraints and she felt herself droop when her wrists were released.

She struggled to stay upright but Carter was there, lifting her in his strong arms. The man was solid and warm. She burrowed against him, needing his strength.

"I've got you, Jenna. Just sleep now," he murmured against her forehead. In this, she chose to trust him, and did as he suggested.

Chapter 4

Jenna awoke with pleasure saturating her system.

"Carter," she said raggedly at the enticing feel of his cock pressed against her rear. The room was shrouded in pre-dawn gray light.

The man was sinful seduction personified. Her world and present existence boiled down to Carter. In his bed, while she lay on her side, Carter spooned her backside and surrounded her body with his larger than life presence. She was cocooned within his embrace, one arm snaked underneath her right side and around to her front where he cupped her left breast. His thumb abraded the nipple, sending torrents of pleasure from her tit directly to her core.

But it was his left arm and, more importantly, his left hand that was the culprit behind waking her up. His fingers stroked through her swollen pussy, caressing her labia, teasing her clitoris. His mouth brushed hungrily against her nape, flicking his tongue against her skin and nipping the sensitive flesh.

Jenna's body was slowly going up in flames from his addictive caresses.

"Sir," she whispered on a jagged moan as he swirled his

fingers around her clit. Yearning for more, needing more, she opened her legs, granting him further access. He nipped at her earlobe.

"Fuck, you're so wet," he murmured, his voice a low growl.

The massive hand cupping her boob pinched and rolled the nipple with his work-roughened fingers, while his other thrummed through her pussy. Just a teasing, erotic caress, no penetration. Need clawed at her. She wanted more, wanted all that he would give her.

Carter rubbed and circled her clit, hitting her pleasure center with a finesse that left her mindless and moaning. The way his body enveloped hers with his larger one, she was at his mercy. Pressed against him, using the teensy bit of wriggle room he left her, she rocked her pelvis, sending what she hoped was a signal that she wanted to ride his fingers. Better yet, that she was done with foreplay entirely and wanted his thick shaft pounding inside her.

His wide erection was snug against her rear. Yet he held her steady, surrounding her with his large body, making it nigh impossible to gain any further friction. All thoughts of resisting him and staying detached slipped away with every sure stroke of his hand through her slit.

Delicious tingles erupted where Carter's shadow beard scraped against her neck and shoulder. She mewled and gasped with every touch, each caress. The man was sensual, magnetic, and inherently attuned to her body. She'd be hard pressed to keep her distance when all she could think about was feeling him inside her again. Then he shifted and rubbed his shaft against her rear.

"Carter," she moaned in a breathy whisper.

He repeated the movement. Jenna's eyes crossed. Flames raged out of control at the sheer intensity of her desire for him. She waged an internal battle. She wanted him—what woman wouldn't want him? Yet she also wanted to resist his animal magnetism. She gripped his arms, her fingers digging into his strong forearms to hold him in place and silently beg him for more.

When he thrust his bulging erection against her rear once more, she begged, "Please, Sir. Please fuck me."

"That's what I want to hear," Carter growled. And then he shifted away.

"Wait, please don't stop." She whined at the loss of his heat, the loss of his body, and the loss of the blissfully sinful caress.

"I just need a condom, darlin', that's all," he replied, his baritone—the deep timbre of it—adding to the eroticism. She loved his husky voice, the way it sounded thick with desire.

"No, you don't. I'm on the pill and I'm clean. Please just fuck me!" she exclaimed, desperate to feel his length inside her. She'd been on the pill for years.

"You're sure?" he murmured, his body completely still behind her.

Exasperated and beyond needy, she whimpered, "Yes, Carter. Sir, just please fuck me!"

He shifted and the bed dipped with his body's movement. He yanked her up against him. She moaned at the re-engaged contact. He spread her thighs, positioning her leg up over his exterior thigh, granting his big body room between her thighs. Jenna squirmed, on edge. Then Carter ran the head of his mammoth shaft through her folds and positioned the crown at the entrance to her sheath. Her pussy quivered in heady anticipation as he penetrated her with just the tip. And then he thrust, hard, plunging his cock inside to the hilt.

"Oh, god!" she cried.

He felt so good, buried deep inside her. Her pussy throbbed around him. Whirls of pleasure spiked her bloodstream. The flames transformed into a wildfire, burning brighter and hotter. And then he began to move, pumping his cock in hard, brutal thrusts. Going so deep, he hit every nerve ending and grazed the lip of her womb. His left hand snaked down to her spread thighs and his fingers caressed her clit, flicking back and forth over the swollen nub. Sparks erupted, adding to the inferno rampant and out of control.

"Christ, you feel like hot velvet squeezing my dick," he growled, his voice husky with desire, then he shifted her face back toward him with his right hand.

Carter slanted his mouth over hers. His kiss was elemental as he methodically screwed her brains right out of her head. He fucked like a man possessed. Like he had been without a woman for years. He was raw, primal lust. And, in that moment, she didn't care one bit as long as he kept fucking her. She loved every minute of his devastating lovemaking. Jenna returned his kiss, showing him with more than words how much she craved him, devolving into a needy creature, wanting nothing but the pleasure he could bring her. The desire he engendered engulfed her, carried her along a tidal wave of intense desire. She parried her tongue against his in a heated, world-altering duel.

She and Carter were connected on every level. Her left hand slid around his nape and threaded into his hair to hold his mouth in place. His lovemaking quite simply decimated her. Called to her on every level of her being. And, deep in the recesses of her soul, recognition registered that this submissive had found her Master.

Jenna's climax hit with all the delicacy of a stampeding herd of elephants. Ecstasy swamped her system. Her pussy spasmed in unending starbursts.

"Carter," she wailed into his mouth while he kept pumping his shaft inside her quaking, clenching sheath.

The man was a machine, rocking his hips until her tremors diminished before sliding his cock from her channel. He lifted his lips and broke their kiss. Then he maneuvered and shifted her onto her stomach. She yelped when he shoved a few pillows under her belly. The pillows elevated her ass up to a forty degree angle. In this position, she was on her knees with her torso flat on the bed. Carter did leave her then, for a moment. And then he was behind her, spreading her legs wide and adding a cool dollop of lubricant to her anus. She hissed when he inserted two fingers in her back channel. It had been a while since she'd had anal and she'd forgotten how good it could feel.

He stretched her, thrusting his lubed fingers inside, adding a third and then a fourth finger. By the time his fingers were gliding unhindered in her ass, Jenna was clutching at the mattress and sheets.

Removing his fingers, he pressed the crown of his shaft against her rosette. He was claiming her, proving that he was large and in charge of her. But Jenna no longer cared. She couldn't deny that she wanted him. His fat, ruddy cock thrust in her back channel. With supreme control, Carter penetrated her little by little until he was buried balls-deep in her ass. Starbursts of pleasure erupted in a fiery tangle. Her pussy throbbed. He shuttled his cock in and out in short, fierce digs, electrifying her core to maddening heights of ecstasy.

His large body pressed hers into the mattress as he pounded his cock in her back channel. Her fingers dug into the sheets as he hammered inside her.

Oh god!

She was coming apart at the seams. He dominated her in every sense of the word, controlled her body, her pleasure, and she reveled in him. In the way he made her feel—so out of control but she knew, deep down, that he would protect her and offer her a soft place to land. Jenna had never felt so over-whelmed by her desire, nor as inherently feminine and submis-sive as she did in that moment.

She gave him what he wanted: her surrender. And she never wanted the mind-numbing lovemaking to end.

Carter's hands gripped the backs of hers on the mattress and he threaded his fingers over hers. He held her, surrounded her, and pummeled her ass with such brutal precision, she couldn't stop the moans. Oh, god. Her body drew taut as her climax neared.

"Sir." She whimpered as pleasure stole her ability to think or reason.

"Come for me Jenna. Come," he ordered on a low growl. The slap of his flesh thumping against hers filled her ears.

She gripped his hands and simply let go, trusting he would take her body where it needed to be. And she was richly rewarded. Carter slammed home and she exploded.

"Carter," she cried at the cataclysmic volts of pleasure that ricocheted through her body. She trembled and quaked in his arms. Her body unraveled for him as she wailed.

"Ah, Jenna. Fuck, yeah!" He bellowed as he strained. His cock poured hot semen into her ass, setting off a secondary round of sparks in her system.

Jenna floated, her body weightless. Carter withdrew from her ass. She moaned as he removed the pillows from beneath her rear. Then he re-arranged her body against his. He lay on his back and pulled her close until she was pillowed up against him, spooning with him once more.

A sense of safety, of security settled over her. It was peaceful and calm, something she hadn't realized she yearned to feel. But it was all there with his solid presence beneath her, his strong arms circling her. As she drifted back to sleep, she imagined she'd felt his knuckles lightly grazing her cheek—as though he cared for her.

But that couldn't be. The big sasquatch only wanted her submission to prove he was a big bad Dom who wouldn't let a sub get the better of him. Right?

Chapter 5

Jenna cracked a bleary eye open to the sunlight streaming in the windows. She was plastered against Carter. The big lug was potent, even while he dreamed. He had fans of inky lashes that most women would kill for. She studied him, glad to have the chance to do so without his piercing hazel eyes that utterly disarmed her or infuriated her with merely a glance. His brows were thick and arched above his expressive eyes. His square jaw was coated with black stubble, framing his wide lips—lips that knew how to kiss her brainless in less than five seconds, like he was some breed of superhuman, or just a really good Dom who knew his way around a woman's body. He looked younger, the lines around his eyes more relaxed as he slept. Granted, that might have been because he'd gotten his rocks off a few times last night screwing her senseless.

At the thought of all the climaxes she'd experienced at his hands, her body purred and turned into a heated mass of need. So much for resisting him. Especially when she'd love to straddle his lap and do very bad things with him, starting with waking him up and riding him. He was a cowboy, she could enact the whole 'save a horse' motto that was popular these days.

With a small groan, she mentally kicked herself. No more hanky-panky with Carter or burrowing back beneath the covers for more shuteye. Jenna didn't have a choice in the matter.

Duty called. Work wouldn't get done on its own. Bills wouldn't get paid if she didn't put one foot in front of the other and do what needed to be done today.

Sliding from his bed, she tiptoed around the villa quietly to retrieve her clothing before she remembered that she didn't have anything but the club blanket to wear back to her place. Wrapping the soft blanket around her shoulders, she escaped Carter's lodge with him none the wiser. Naked, asleep, Carter looked so much more inviting than she wished he did.

Wearing nothing but the blanket, Jenna did the island equivalent of the walk of shame. Although, if she was honest, she didn't regret last night. She may not have appreciated how she got there, but the end result had been quite simply the best sex of her life. She had to hand it to the sasquatch, he had rendered her brainless more than once and given her a boatload of orgasms.

In her apartment, she took a speedy shower while gulping coffee down to help fuel herself for the day ahead. Her cart was parked at the main hotel. Of course. Which meant she had to hot foot it across the island to get her day started on time. She was in and out of her apartment in under thirty minutes. She didn't bother with drying her hair as the heat would take care of it for her, but had it scraped back into a high ponytail to keep it out of the way. Besides, in the humidity here, just like in her home state of Florida, her hair refused to behave, preferring to frizz and curl. So she tended to have it pulled back ninety percent of the time. And Doms loved a long ponytail so it was win-win.

Jenna reached the main hotel wondering why she'd bothered to take a shower at all, other than to remove the dried semen between her thighs—she was sweating and her day had barely begun. Already there were a myriad number of errands that required her assistance. At least it was easy work, and for the pay, she couldn't complain.

Her morning sped by before she realized it was midday and she'd not stopped to eat yet. She had one more errand to run to the docks before she could take a lunch break. She exited the hotel, paying attention to the boxed lunches for the boat captains and not necessarily minding her surroundings.

In her defense, the man—for all his size—moved with the stealth of a panther and was bearing down on her. Anger seethed from him and his face could have been made from granite as he glared at her.

What had she done this time? Sometimes she wondered if she just pissed people off by merely existing.

"Where the hell have you been?" Carter snarled as he approached.

She raised a brow and gave him this *well, duh* glance, indicating what she carried in her hands and said, "At work. Look, I have to run these to the docks and get them to Derek and Shep."

"Your job this week is me," Carter said with possessiveness and finality, brooking no room for argument on her part.

Instead of kicking him in his very large shins, she huffed. "No, it's not. Just because I'm submitting to you this week doesn't mean I don't have to work, Carter."

He growled. "As your punishment—"

"Which I've already paid back in spades at this point for a minor infraction, Sir. I have to go. I will be back at your villa tonight and then you can have at it, all right?" she said, gesturing with a nod at her body.

"I'll pay you. So then you don't have to work this week," he snapped.

She flinched like he'd struck her. Pay her. The man wanted to pay her to sleep with her. Jenna was a lot of things and had many faults, but she would never fuck someone for money and wasn't about to start now. Her voice scathing, she replied,

"Screw you, Carter. Do us both a favor and head back to Montana."

"It's Wyoming. And I'm not sure what the big deal is—"

"Which is precisely why you can go fuck yourself," she retorted, spitting mad and seeing red. Before she did something terrible, like castrate the asshole, she hot-footed it away from him. She was certain de-manning a guest would surely get her fired.

JENNA WORKED the early shift at the club and debated with herself whether or not she should even go back to Carter's lodge as she finished her shift. She was exhausted after today. A part of her wanted to give him the proverbial finger, head back to her apartment and lonely bed. But that course of action was reckless and wouldn't be worth the momentary satisfaction of thumbing her nose at him should he report her dismissal to her boss. Rock and hard place were some of her best friends.

In the end, a saner head prevailed. She needed the job on the island. If she refused and Carter lodged a protest with Jared, she was sunk. To make the kind of money she did on the island, she'd have to work three jobs back home in Tampa.

She'd go to Carter's, but hell if she was having sex with him tonight. And that was a non-negotiable line of demarcation. If he protested, she would be the one to lodge a complaint with Jared.

Her footsteps dragged as she got onto the elevator. Her feet ached from running around on them all day. Jenna rode the elevator up. The door slid open and she straightened her spine. Carter sat like a pissed off overlord on the leather chair in the living room. His face was as hard as granite, his gaze like razor blades as she entered.

"Strip and kneel," he ordered in a clipped voice.

"No." She refused his command, her hands going to her hips in a rebellious stance. She defied him with fury of her own bubbling to the surface.

"You're really asking for a punishment today, aren't you, darlin? Do you like being disciplined, is that it?" he asked quietly, barely moving a muscle. For all his control, his energy was like that of a panther ready to spring on its prey.

"No. I don't like being compared to a whore and a prostitute. I won't kneel or whatever the hell else you had planned for tonight," she replied.

He shook his head and said, "I never compared you to that."

She shifted her body, crossing her arms in front of her chest and murmured, "Oh, so you didn't offer to pay me to fuck you this week? Would you like me to provide you with the definition of prostitute? Because that's what you turned me into today. If that's what you're looking for, I'm not it and I will leave now."

His expression was contrite but then the sasquatch opened his mouth. "Darlin', I didn't mean to make it sound that way. But you overstepped—"

"I don't care what fucking Dom rule I overstepped or boundary I crossed, you hurt me. You turned what we did last night into something cheap, and turned me into a whore. And no, we are not okay. I am not okay with what you said today. And nothing you can say or do right now will make it right. If you have any measure of respect for me at all, you will leave me be. I've had an incredibly long day and am taking a hot bath—alone, thank you. Then I plan on sleeping on the couch tonight. If you fight me on this, I walk, Carter," she said, not minding her tone or watching her tongue. Then she walked past the living room— and him. She'd said her piece. The rest was up to him.

When she reached the door to the bathroom she sensed him at her back. She swiveled and said, "What?"

"I truly did not mean it that way, Jenna, and for that I am sorry. I can be difficult and like things a certain way. I will give you tonight. But then we will discuss our arrangement in the morning," he said.

"Our arrangement. You mean the one where if I don't submit to you this week, I lose my job? Like I have a choice in the matter," she murmured and shut the door in his face. As she gave the lock a firm twist, she felt her shoulders sag at the sound of the mechanism latching.

FUCK!

Carter grimaced as he let himself out on the back deck. It was either that or stare at the firmly shut bathroom door. She'd locked him out. Not that he blamed her. He had been an ass. And he hadn't meant what he'd said to her earlier to come off the way it had. Or perhaps a part of him had, as a way to maintain his distance from her. She tended to bring out his caveman instincts—which, on a good day, were rather daunting to say the least.

He hadn't expected to care. But he'd never meant to cause her harm. And damn, but he didn't want her with him if her job was riding on it. That was something he could resolve right away.

Pulling out his cell phone, he dialed Jared's number.

"Carter, is something amiss?" Jared asked.

"No. Nothing's wrong. I just wanted to let you know that as far as I'm concerned, Jenna has met the terms of her punishment with me."

"Did she do something wrong? Or is she—"

"Jared she's fine." *For the most part.* "Moving forward, I don't want her to be required to be with me. Her employment with you remains intact whether she stays with me the rest of this week or not—her job on the island does not hinge on that fact. Understood?" he said.

"Ah, I see," Jared said, sounding bemused. The fucker. "Anything else I can do for you this evening, Carter?"

"Nope. We're good."

"That's fine then. And I will consider Jenna's punishment at an end. Enjoy the rest of your night," Jared said, a laugh in his Scottish voice.

"Yep," he said and hung up before he did something stupid, like drive over to the hotel just to pummel the man to make himself feel better.

When he headed back inside, Jenna was making up the couch for herself wearing a tank top that said 'Bite Me' across the chest, and pajama bottoms with the word 'juicy' across her fine ass. He bit back a grin. She was such a fascinating mix of righteous determination and independence. Then, tossed in for good measure, was an inherent desire to please. Not to mention that all he had to do was smell her scent—jasmine and vanilla—and he grew rock hard. Their chemistry was off the charts combustible.

"Enjoy your bath?" he asked.

"I did, thank you. Good night, Sir," she said, not looking at him as she settled onto the couch and snuggled underneath the blankets.

"Good night, Jenna." He grabbed a beer from the fridge, and then he sat in the armchair and watched her sleep.

Normally she was a dynamo of energy that infiltrated and surrounded the space she occupied. Seeing her all curled up, he thought she looked so small and delicate. Breakable. An emotion he'd long ago thought himself incapable of feeling again surged inside his chest: the need to protect. More often than not, he enjoyed a sub at the club, but never allowed them into his personal space or got bent out of shape when they chose another Dom after being with him. One who didn't hold his emotions back.

But Christ, she made him want more, not to just tame her

and have a good time. Carter wanted to possess her, wanted her to belong to him, wanted to erase the exhaustion he'd seen in her eyes tonight and care for her. If he wasn't careful, he'd end up wanting a whole lot more with her, and he didn't know if that was wise.

Man, but she kept him on his toes. She was submissive, absolutely, because when she was beneath him, she was his every fantasy brought to life. Although, she wasn't coy or shy in the slightest, and did not take crap from anyone, most especially him. He'd never had a woman challenge him the way she did. Which was a stark change. Usually, at his club, the submissives rarely spoke above a whisper, never looked him in the eye, and assumed whatever position he requested without question or hesitation.

Jenna was a breath of fresh air he hadn't known he needed.

When her soft snores reached his ears, he set his empty bottle on the coffee table and stood. Bending down, he hoisted her slight form into his arms. No way in hell was his sub sleeping on the couch.

And then she snuggled against his chest as he carried her, and pleasure speared him at the innocent unconscious gesture.

Carter laid her on the bed and drew the covers up over her. He stroked her head, his fingers tangling in her hair. She truly was enchanting.

He left her in the bed and went throughout the lodge, turning off lights before he stripped out of his jeans and boxer briefs, then slid into bed alongside her. Carter gathered her close.

At her innocuous sigh, his chest loosened. Her head was now pillowed on his chest and he looked down at her stunning face. She fit him. Perhaps she didn't see it yet and, well, he wasn't comfortable with it, but she did.

And wasn't that the most surprising event so far—her advent into his world? Now he just had to figure out how to keep her there.

Chapter 6

J enna stretched as the loveliest aromas assailed her senses. Coffee and some delicious meat. She blinked her eyes open only to realize she was in bed. Carter's bed. His spicy woodsy scent on the sheets beside her. She'd fallen asleep on the couch. Which meant Carter had moved her over there sometime last night. And she slept like the freaking dead, typically, because she was always exhausted. So the fact that he didn't wake her up as he moved her from the couch to the bed wasn't a huge surprise.

What did astonish her, though, was that he had cared enough to see to her comfort by transferring her from one place to the other. And that her heart trembled and sighed at his actions. When was the last time anyone had cared about her comfort? She was the one who took care of everyone else.

It had been such a long stretch of time since, that Jenna couldn't actually remember when someone else had taken care of her last.

"Good morning," Carter said, his back still turned to her while he was at the stove. What, did that man have eyes in the back of his head?

"Morning," she replied, her voice dry and raspy.

"There's coffee if you'd like. Eggs will be ready in a minute," he murmured, still with his back to her. She approached the kitchen. For such a large man, he moved with ease and grace. And seeing he was wearing nothing but a pair of black boxers made her want to take a bite out of him. Sweet heavens, but even from behind the man packed a powerful punch. He was made of one hundred percent pure muscle. There wasn't an ounce of fat on him.

She shuffled over to the coffee pot, weary and wondering just what he was up to.

At the first sip of coffee, her eyes widened. And she'd thought she liked *her* coffee dark and strong. Carter's version would put the balls back on a bull. There were plates arranged on the kitchen island and she slid onto one of the stools.

Then he turned with the frying pan in hand and added eggs to her plate before doing the same with the plate beside hers. Not saying anything, he moved a plate full of crispy bacon and toast over near their plates. Then he strode around the island and sat on the stool beside her.

"Eat, before it gets cold," he said, a hint of command in his voice.

She just stared at him. What was he up to? And then he slid bacon and a piece of toast onto her plate. He'd cooked her breakfast. Was this his way of making amends, or buttering her up?

"What? Why aren't you eating?" he asked with a raised brow.

"What are you playing at?" she asked, unable to keep the wariness out as it colored her voice.

"At feeding you, Jenna. Eat," he commanded.

Still not fully trusting the situation, she did as he asked and discovered she was starving. It had been so long since she hadn't been the one who had to forage for food. Normally her breakfasts consisted of opening the cereal box and pouring it into a bowl. So this, having him cook breakfast—and a really good one at that—made her blink back tears.

His hand caressed her back. "Relax, Jenna, it's just breakfast."

Oh but it wasn't. It was far more than that. It was sneaky and underhanded, and she hated to admit it, but just about the nicest thing anyone had done for her in a long time. She nodded, blinking back the moisture in her eyes. Then she ate every damn crumb on her plate.

When she'd finished she sighed at her full belly and glanced over to find him studying her.

"Thank you, Sir," she said, giving him a small smile.

"Hasn't anyone ever made breakfast for you?" he asked, observing her intently.

She shook her head. "No, not since I was a little girl and my mom was alive. Why?"

"Just curious is all," he replied.

She took a sip of coffee, feeling the jolt of caffeine in the potent brew hit her bloodstream.

Carter stated, very matter-of-factly, his visage serious, "About our arrangement: you're free to choose."

She choked on her coffee. Her eyes watered and she cleared her throat. Then she said, "I'm sorry. I'm not sure I understand."

"I've already talked to Jared. Your punishment is finished. You don't have to stay with me unless you choose to do so," he said, his face unreadable.

"Why? Why would you do that?" she asked. She was in completely unfamiliar terrain. Carter had ended her punishment early? She didn't understand why he would do such a thing. He wanted her to stay with him.

He gave her a hard stare before responding. "Because you were right, it wasn't fair to you that your employment hinged on being with me this week. That's not how I want you. If you're going to be with me, I want it to be of your own free will. All you have to do is say yes."

Jenna gazed at him, trying to figure him out. He wanted her. No strings, no conditions, just her saying yes and admitting that she wanted to be with him this week. Her pulse thumped. She didn't know what to say. Truth be told, a part of her wanted to respond with an unequivocal yes, while the more cautious and her admittedly wary nature wanted her to hold back.

"Why, Carter? Why do you want me this week?" she asked, her voice raw with emotion.

He swiveled her body on the stool then so she was facing him. Put his hands on either side of the stool beneath her rump and boxed her in. His hazel gaze bored into hers as he said, "Because I think there's something here between us—whether it's just an itch that needs scratching, or more, I'd like to find out. When I say I want you in particular, I mean it."

"But you can have any sub on the island."

He shrugged, his massive shoulders rippling enticingly with the subtle movement. "I don't want the other subs on the island. I want you. Period. Now, the question is, why is this such a hard decision? Either you want me or you don't."

"And if I say yes, what then? What happens at the end of the week?" she pressed him.

"We go our separate ways, or we work something else out. By then, you could be sick of me and ready to be rid of me."

But that was her fear. That she would say yes and have to let him go. Just like she'd had to do with everything else in her life. Jenna didn't know if she could stand losing one more thing. Except… if it was her choice, couldn't she make the decision here and now that if she chose to be with him for the rest of this week, she would make it be enough?

Wanting to test her theory, since she wasn't on a subspace high, she cupped his face in her hands. His stubble prickled and scraped against her palms. She leaned forward, her eyes on him. And he watched her, waiting for her to make her decision. Closing the remaining distance between them, she placed her mouth over his and kissed him. Brushing her lips against his, she learned their shape. She sucked his bottom lip, enjoying his taste, flavored like the dark coffee he'd brewed. Then she flicked her tongue and sought entrance into his mouth.

He granted her that, but still he didn't touch her except with his mouth and tongue. She caressed the inside of his mouth with hers, sliding her tongue inside, and she knew, right then and there, what her answer was. Her hands slid around to the back of his neck and she took the kiss deeper. With that he finally put his hands on her and lifted her off the stool so that she was straddling him. Her body rejoiced at the contact.

She moaned into his mouth as he took over control of their kiss. It was a claiming as he slanted his mouth over hers. A possession, telling her with his caress that she belonged to him. And she reveled in it. Jenna plastered herself around his big, hard body.

He was her choice.

Carter finally broke their torrid kiss, his gaze blazing with lust, and said, "I'm assuming that's a yes."

"Yes." She nodded, panting.

"Thank Christ. You have five minutes. Then I want you naked and in my bed," he said, the command inherent in his voice while his hands palmed her butt.

Her stomach fluttered, and she nodded. "I have to be at work at five tonight."

"Then that should be just enough time." He winked as he set her down on her feet. His playful demeanor, combined with this morning's events, had shoved her world on its axis, so much so that her knees wobbled.

She took the time allotted to run to the bathroom to use the facilities and strip before walking back into the room in the buff.

As she climbed into bed, Carter was at the armoire withdrawing a few items.

Jenna lay back on the bed, and spread her legs wide. When Carter turned and spied her, a hungry, predatory smirk appeared on his face.

"Now that's about the loveliest sight I've seen all week," he murmured, moving around the bed. He fastened the cuffs on her wrists to black nylon rope with silver loops at the ends and then attached Velcro straps around her ankles. Now she was spread-eagle as Carter joined her. He positioned himself between her thighs. His mighty erection jutted from his hips as he leaned over her, holding himself up by his elbows. This position lined their bodies up from shoulders to hips. She melted at the heady contact, the feel of his firmness pressed up against her.

Carter's hands framed her face, lifting her gaze to his and he said, "Now, I want you to come as many times as you need to. This is about me learning your sweet body, starting with your gorgeous tits. Understood?"

"Yes, Sir," she replied, unable to keep the soft moan from her voice.

He lowered his face and claimed her mouth, taking his time seducing her with merely his lips. Light kisses that made her insides melt into a fluffy marshmallow. Soft, lingering ones that sent her head spinning and yearning for more. And then ravenous, hungry kisses that shattered her composure and left her begging for more. Then he held himself aloft, close enough that she could feel his body heat and yet far enough away that she couldn't feel him.

Carter lifted his head. When she lifted hers off the pillow and tried to recapture his lips, he cast her a wicked grin, like he knew exactly how much she enjoyed his kisses and precisely how much they made her ache for more.

He trailed open-mouthed kisses over her collarbone and the sensitive hollow at the base of her throat. Tendrils of heat slid through her veins. Carter continued his sensual exploration down the slope of her chest to her breasts. He curled his tongue around one distended bud and tugged. She moaned as he fastened his lips over the bud, laving her nipple. His hands massaged the plump mounds, learning their shape and size, testing the weight of the globes. His mouth traveled over the mounds, biting and sucking on her flesh until her nipples spiked into hard beaded points. Whirls of delicious, illicit pleasure spiked her blood and made her pussy throb in sheer agonized anticipation.

She wanted him. Now. Except, she never wanted the spine-tingling pleasure to end. And then he moved yet again, placing kisses over her belly, nipping at her hip bones, until his head was between her spread thighs.

"Christ, you're so fucking wet." He moaned and lowered his mouth to her pussy. At the first swipe of his tongue through her folds, Jenna's head fell back. Carter ate her pussy without preamble, sucking at her hole, flicking his tongue against her clit with a fervent ardor that drove her body right up and over the edge, eliciting toe-curling pleasure.

"Oh, Sir!" She screamed as she came. Her body trembled and quaked. Yet Carter didn't stop. If anything, he amped up his campaign. His tongue thrust in and out. Her moans filled the villa as he pressed two lube-coated fingers against her anus.

As he penetrated her rear, he vigorously ate her pussy. She could smell the musky scent of their love play. Carter began thrusting his arm in a sawing motion. Jenna's moans grew louder, echoing in the room. Her sex gripped at his tongue plunging in time to his fingers thrusting in her back channel. Her clit swelled from his fervent ministrations.

He lifted his face from her pussy and turned his head, her cream coating his black stubble beard, and growled over his shoulder, "Either join us or leave now."

Then he moved until he was kneeling before her and turned back to her as he poured more lubricant into his hand. He shoved his boxers down and she almost came at the sight. Circling his cock and balls was a cock ring with a beaded protrusion that he slicked lube over. Then he positioned his cock at the entrance to her pussy and the beaded dildo at her back channel so that just the tips were inserted. His fierce gaze held hers and then he thrust forward with a roll of his pelvis. Jenna moaned as he filled her.

Oh, my god! He was so big, and the added element of double penetration took her out of this world. She knew there was someone in the villa with them but she didn't care. She was too far gone in the sea of pleasure that was Carter.

When he was fully embedded, he glanced over his shoulder again. His hips rocked and rolled, pounding away inside her channels, and snarled, "Either get that pussy of yours over here with your thighs spread and ready for my cock, or get the fuck out."

Then his attention swiveled back to her. Whoever had been in the villa must have left.

"What other pussy do you want besides mine?" she gasped, needing to know. She clutched at the rope restraints as waves of pleasure swamped her, her body engulfed in tidal waves of flames.

"Hush now, darlin', I only said that to shock the little maid. Seems she was enjoying watching me fuck you. And the only pussy I want is currently enveloping my cock like heated fucking silk." He grunted and slammed his hips down.

"Oh," she whimpered as pleasure cascaded through her with his thrusts.

He crowded her with his body, holding himself up on his elbows as he thrust hard and so deep she practically saw stars. Her gaze was heavy-lidded as she stared at him, her mouth agape, unable to hold back her moans.

Jenna unraveled as she came. Her body shuddered and her pussy quaked. Yet still Carter thrust, proving that he intended to use every drop of energy and time at his disposal today. Sweat slicked their bodies as he pounded her pussy and ass.

"Please let me touch you," she begged, straining against her wrist restraints. He never stopped fucking her as he undid first one and then the other.

But his control began to slip as her hands slid over his broad shoulders. He pistoned his hips, pushing her body up a cliff of pleasure. Jenna came again, screaming his name as his tempo increased and he unleashed his control, burying his face in the crook of her neck. She held him close as he hammered inside her.

The world coalesced into bright, shiny exploding stars as her pussy and ass erupted in a climax so profound it launched her body off planet.

"Carter," she wailed.

He stiffened in her arms. His cock plunged, and hot streams of semen filled her quaking sheath. "Jenna," he roared in her ear, thrusting like mad as his seed filled her.

He lay supine over her, still buried balls deep inside her. They were both breathing heavily as their heartrates returned to normal. She thrilled at the feeling of his weight on top of her. The way her body cradled the hard planes of his and how he held her close.

As if she mattered.

It was a pipe dream. She knew that. But she let herself imagine it was real. It wouldn't hurt, right?

Then Carter leaned up on his elbows, his handsome face inches from hers as she opened her eyes. His gaze searched hers and she didn't know what he sought or what he saw when he looked at her. His thumb traced her lower lip.

And then he lowered his mouth, brushed his lips over hers tenderly, and she had to fight back the tears. As fierce and as heated as their lovemaking tended to become, it was this, right here, that moved her more than anything.

Then he withdrew his semi-hard shaft and the beaded dildo. He moved about, undoing her ankle restraints and then left her on the bed. Which was fine. She could barely lift her limbs and could feel the edges of her consciousness slipping.

He returned with a warm washcloth and cleaned her up between her legs. When he'd finished, he pulled the bedcovers up over her.

"Sleep," he ordered, and turned to leave her alone in his bed. But she shot her hand out and placed it on his strong forearm.

"Don't leave me," she said, her voice a hesitant whisper.

Carter glanced at her hand, his expression tender, then tossed the washcloth onto the nightstand. He slid in beside her and gathered her close. "Wouldn't dream of it, darlin'."

She snuggled against his firm chest and shut her eyes, not questioning her actions or potential consequences for once in her life. Just enjoying being surrounded and held by Carter.

Chapter 7

Carter was more relaxed than he had been in an age as he got himself prepared for a hike around the island while awaiting Jenna's return.

She was the reason his stress levels had plummeted. There was no other explanation for it. And not one of his orgasms with her had been perfunctory—rather, epic and world-altering. Carter was an experienced Master and had been with his fair share of submissives, but not one of them had ever engendered this much relaxation and simple deep in the bone satisfaction.

Which meant the calm and peace he felt was her. She did something to him.

Jenna was fiercely independent, wildly intelligent, and a damn hard worker. Perhaps it was that combination, along with her shocked pleasure over yesterday morning's breakfast. Or the way she clutched at him after sex, asking him not to leave, like she didn't want to let him go, that continued to capture his attention.

It didn't hurt that the sex between them was on the next level. Jenna was a rare jewel of a submissive—open and willing to accede to a Dom's every wish and fantasy.

At least in bed.

Her defiance was just another one of those things about her that seemed to fuel his hunger and lust for her. That she could be so circumspect and unwilling to back down as she went toe to toe with him. Yet it made her surrender beneath his hands all the more captivating, not to mention getting the chance to swat her cute ass.

If he were a believer in the occult, he'd say she had ensorcelled him.

The elevator door opened and pleasure seeped into his soul. He turned and was sucker punched at her beauty. She'd braided her hair this morning and golden wisps had escaped while she'd been out, framing her beautiful face. But it was her eyes that drew him in. Those large cornflower blue orbs were expressive. She hid what she felt in every line of her body but her eyes gave her away. And they were looking at him now with heat and consternation.

His little sub appeared to be as confounded by their connection as he.

"How was work?" he asked.

"Long," she replied, a hint of exhaustion in her voice.

"If you don't want to go, we don't have to. We can stay here."

"No. I do, but would you mind if we stop at my apartment? I need some things," she said, approaching him.

"Yeah. What things do you need?" he asked, tugging her the rest of the way until he had her in his arms.

"Well, for one, I'm running out of clean clothing."

"Since you're not wearing them here, I don't see how that's a problem," he replied.

"Let me rephrase that: attire for work so that I'm not having to constantly run from here to my place to change and then try to make it across the island for my shift," she said.

He hadn't realized that was what she'd been doing. Christ,

there was a lot about her he didn't know. He knew precisely what it took to send her body over the edge of ecstasy, but otherwise he had no idea about her.

"Ah, well. While I think you should always be naked, I can see how that's an issue. Let's get a move on," he said.

She was studying him intently, her gaze burning into him.

"What?" he asked.

"You just look different without your jeans and cowboy boots, that's all. I like it, I just didn't expect you to own something that wasn't jeans," she teased.

"Well now, darlin', just because I live and work on a ranch doesn't mean my wardrobe is strictly that. You've not seen me in leather pants either," he responded. He realized the tank top and basketball shorts were not his typical gear, but it was hotter than blue blazes outside. While he lived and worked outdoors, in rain, snow, bitter cold or scorching heat, the humidity here was a killer.

Her gaze traveled over his body and he felt it all the way down to his sneakers. "I'd like to see that."

He leaned down and nipped her bottom lip. "That can be arranged."

Carter ran his knuckles down her cheek and she leaned in to his caress. Her fingers curled into his chest. Her passionate gaze sucked him in and pulled him under. Her forthright stare was filled with desire and hunger yet he spied more, something deeper, and it rocked him. Then she blinked, broke the heated spell as she retreated, and said, "Maybe when we return, big guy. We should get going before it gets too much hotter today."

She disentangled herself from his hold and he let her, wholly unprepared for the emotions she engendered inside him. "Certainly."

He escorted her out of his lodgings, enjoying the way the sun illuminated her tan skin and golden tresses. They headed off in the cart, with Jenna pointing out various locations. Trails that could take them to the greenhouse or the airstrip.

The westward side of the island was less tame. Other than the set of apartment buildings on one corner, the rest was wild and unspoiled. He loved that. It reminded him more of his ranch; the open expanse of land remote and natural.

Carter followed Jenna into her first-floor apartment. The pre-furnished dwelling was not overly large, and contained furniture and a design similar to those in the villas. But there were touches of her everywhere; bright candles, a vase on the pinewood dining table with flowers that looked like she had picked them from the island. It smelled like her, that unique, exotic jasmine fragrance. Jenna's place was little more than a studio apartment with an open floor plan. A queen-sized bed covered with ivory sheets stood across from the living room with a single leather sofa and chair. Beside her television stand was a small desk with a tablet computer. He checked out her place as she moved around the same way she did everything—as if she were a tornado, opening her dresser and closet and tossing items into a bag.

There were picture frames she'd hung on the walls near her desk. Candid shots of her with another blonde. She seemed younger, but her features were similar enough in appearance form him to guess that they had to be related. Then there was one with an older gentleman, his hair fully white but his eyes the same as Jenna's as he smiled into the camera.

"My father, Dale," Jenna said beside him.

"And who's this?" he asked, pointing at the one with the other blonde.

"My sister, Meghan. That was taken a few years ago, at a birthday party, if I remember correctly."

"She seems young," he commented.

"And I'm not, is that what you're saying?" she asked with a spark of fire in her gaze.

"No. Not at all. You just... ah, hell—"

"Relax, big guy, I'm just yanking your chain. She's six years younger than me. Mom and Dad had trouble conceiving so she was a surprise baby for them after years of trying," she murmured.

"And what about your mom? You don't have any recent photos of her up," he said and saw her entire demeanor change.

"She died when I was young," Jenna said, but her lips were compressed. A slash of pain flashed in her gaze briefly before she replaced it with a bland smile that didn't reach her eyes.

"I'm sorry. Both of my parents died a few years back. I know it's something you never truly get over. Once my mom passed, dad just couldn't seem to continue living without her and died in his sleep," Carter said, giving her waist a squeeze.

"It depends on the manner in which they choose to leave and whether it was from natural causes," she murmured and then tried to turn away from him.

"What do you mean by that? Talk to me, Jenna, how did your mom die?"

"Suicide. I was eight. Meghan was only two at the time," she said, her voice a pained whisper.

"Jesus, Jenna. Sorry doesn't begin to cut it." He wrapped her in his arms. She sighed brokenly against him, fisting her hands in his shirt and burying her face in his chest. It was clear that this was sore spot. One that, if they had more time together, he would draw out of her. As it was, he didn't want to make her sad and prod at a scar that obviously still hurt her.

"It happened a long time ago," she murmured, muffled against his chest.

"I'm still sorry for it," he mumbled against her temple.

"It's fine. Can we get out of here?" she asked, shifting her head to look up at him, her gaze beseeching.

"Absolutely," he replied. Carter looped her bag over his shoulder and then escorted her back to the cart. He wanted to put excitement back in her eyes and make her smile again.

In the cart, he asked, "Where should we go from here?"

"Um, get back on the path and then take the first left. You can't come to the island and not see the view from the overlook," she said.

He did as she suggested, watching her from the corner of his eye as he drove them over the path. It ascended in gentle waves, the verdant green jungle vegetation lining the path.

"So what do you do, Carter?"

"I own a ranch outside of Jackson Hole, Wyoming," he replied and cast a glance her way.

"And what do you do on your ranch?"

"Breed and raise quarter horses."

"Really? What's that like?" she asked.

"A lot of hard work, early mornings spent waking before the sun even crests the horizon. But it's good, honest work and I can't imagine doing anything else. Have you ever ridden?" he asked her, thinking she'd make quite the picture astride one of his mares.

"A horse? No. We didn't have extra for frivolities like that."

"Well if you ever get a hankering for it, I'd be happy to teach you," he murmured.

"Maybe. One day. I don't know that I see myself leaving the island anytime soon. Unfortunately," she muttered and then blushed at the admission.

"You don't like it here, on the island?" he asked, surprised by her response. Yet it also planted the seed of an idea.

"No, I do," she said hastily.

"But?" There was no way he was letting her out of this one. If she was unhappy here, he wanted to know why, for a number of reasons.

"There's a difference between wanting to be at a place and needing to, is all. My life hasn't been my own, well, not for twenty years or so. It doesn't matter anyway. It's here where I am and here where I will stay," she said and looked in the opposite direction.

Twenty years or so, which meant ever since her mother had passed. He couldn't imagine growing up with that specter, that ghost crowding everything one did. His parents, while not perfect, had never made him doubt for one second that they loved him. Wanting to diffuse the lines of tension in her, he said, "You should come for a visit. You can relax on the back patio with a cup of coffee with a clear view of the Grand Tetons. Not to diss on the mountain here, but there's nothing quite like the mountains back home."

"You love it there," she said.

"Yeah, I do. It's about forty-five minutes or so from downtown Jackson Hole. There's not the hustle of the big cities. And you can see the stars come out every night."

"It sounds nice."

"It is. Now there's a sight you don't see every day," he murmured, pulling up near the abutment. There was one of the outdoor stations that had been erected. And, out beyond that, from this precipice, one could see the beach and ocean beyond.

"It's my favorite spot here. Up away from everyone. I don't have to worry about anything and can just be," Jenna said rather wistfully.

There were layers of herself that she was hiding. It went deeper than just her mother's suicide. He rubbed a hand down her back, wanting to replace her frown with happiness and pleasure. Christ, she made him want to stand as her guardian, protect her from whatever it was that put that helpless look on her face.

"Want to make it an even better spot?" he asked, giving her a seductive grin.

She shifted her gaze to his. He thrilled at her audible intake of breath as he watched her pupils dilate and her pale pink tongue dart out to wet her bottom lip.

"How?" she asked.

"Do you trust me?"

"Yes, Sir," she replied.

And Carter knew, coming from this woman with her fierce independence and simmering passion, that was a victory.

"Good. Come with me," he murmured, the hint of command in his voice.

Carter led her over to the overlook station, replete with a padded leather fuck bench: one of his favorites, as it put a sub at his mercy.

When they reached the bench, he directed, "Disrobe for me."

While she slid out of the short shorts, tank top and her lingerie—which made him hard as a rock to see every time, as she was pure perfection—he went to the small waterproof trunk and withdrew some ankle restraints.

He headed back over to her. She was submissive in every cell in her body, but she was also defiant as hell and stood proud, her head up and gaze on him. He didn't know if she would ever truly submit fully. But Christ, he wanted to be the one she gifted with it.

He tugged her into his arms, his hand on her nape, tilting her face toward his. Carter claimed her mouth, his tongue invading her warm recesses. He kissed her unleashing his primitive caveman, who wanted nothing more than to claim her, mark her as his. Jenna's hands slid up his chest and he felt the caress down to the soles of his feet. Her hands scorched a trail up to grip the back of his neck, making her press her hot fucking body against him.

He growled into her mouth at the feel of her breasts pressed against his chest. He was drowning in Jenna. Grenades could be exploding around them and he wouldn't know it—or care, for that matter. She took him out of his headspace, made the rest of the world recede, and shredded the very foundation of his vaunted control.

By the time he ended the kiss, it was he who was trembling,

he who felt perilously close to murmuring words that he wasn't ready to utter. He wanted to keep her, wanted her to belong to him.

His breathing was heavy as he stared at her. And the desire blazing in her gaze nearly brought him to his knees. She was precious to him as he lifted her up, then proceeded to strap her on her hands and knees to the bench. It gave him a deep in the bone thrill that his cuffs were on her wrists.

What bowled him over was that he wanted them to stay there permanently. He couldn't remember the last time he'd had the urge to claim a submissive as his. It had been years. But one look at Jenna restrained on the horse and a part of him simply decreed: mine.

He caressed her cheek with a finger and said, "Just pleasure with this session, darlin', but use your safeword if you need to."

"Yes, Sir," she murmured.

Carter walked around to her tail end. The pretty puffy lips of her pussy glistened with dew. He couldn't help himself. He had to taste her. He bent down on one knee. With his hands he spread her folds farther apart, then tongued her slit from her clit all the way to her anus.

At Jenna's sharp cry of pleasure, he grinned, then latched his mouth around her clit, flicking the nub with measured strokes. He loved the way she tasted. And at the little mewls she made when he plunged his tongue inside her pussy, he felt pre-cum seep from his rock-hard erection.

"Carter," she moaned. The breathy sound went straight to his cock and made it twitch.

As much as he wanted to slam inside her and feel her heat envelop his dick, he wanted to send her body over the edge first. Carter ate her pussy, driving her body toward climax. He reveled in her moans and the way she cried his name.

He bit down on the bud and she screamed. He felt her pussy

contract around his tongue as he thrust inside and lapped at her cream. And then he couldn't wait anymore.

He strode around toward the front of the bench, throwing off his tank top as he went, until he stood before her. Carter shoved his shorts and boxers down, exposing his cock. Her heated gaze caused more cum to leak from his crown.

"Open up for me, darlin'," he said through gritted teeth, his dick fisted in one hand while he cupped her head with the other. He didn't have to ask her twice. Jenna's mouth dropped open wide and he inserted the head. He hissed at the way her tongue caressed his crest, lapping up the pre-cum with relish. She swished her tongue around the tip playfully before she closed her lips around him like a vise grip and suctioned his shaft inside her mouth.

He thrust, loving the feel of her surrounding him. Jenna was a vision, strapped on all fours, as he stuffed his cock in her wet heat. She moaned around his dick, obviously as aroused as he was. Carter pumped his hips, his hands cradling her head as he rammed his dick between her lips.

The way she sucked his cock—hollowing her cheeks and then, when he was deep inside, sucking his member hard—nothing could drag him away. And her hot little mouth was ripping his control to smithereens. But he didn't want to come there.

He withdrew his erection from her eager lips. At her needy whimper, pleasure speared him.

He walked around Jenna's restrained form until he was between her thighs. Lining up the head of his cock, he stroked it over her drenched folds. Then Carter drove his erection inside Jenna.

"Oh god," she screamed and climaxed around his shaft.

Her pussy clasped around his cock and he held still, waiting for her flutters to subside. His hands went to her hips as he started shuttling his length in and out. Hot fucking silk gripped his dick and nearly made his knees buckle at the pleasure. Carter's beast clamored to the forefront and slashed at his composure as he thrust.

He wanted to imprint himself on her. Make her body know who its true Master was and be the one she craved.

Carter fucked her, jackhammering his shaft inside her, violently pumping his pelvis with brutal force. Jenna's cries of ecstasy spurred his beast on. He dug his fingers into her hips as he shuttled his cock inside her. Jenna wailed in a frenzy.

She canted her hips as much as the restraints would allow and met his thrusts, obviously craving release. Carter withdrew his erection from Jenna's pussy. Pouring lube over his cock, he placed the tip at her back hole. Jenna bucked, going wild, and he worked his fat cock inside her ass.

He loved this sight, seeing his erection disappear inside her ass. The sounds Jenna emitted were nearly animalistic. He felt his control slip with every thrust of his cock inside her taut channel.

He smacked her ass and Jenna keened, "Carter."

Then she was coming, her ass squeezing his cock in hard spasms as she came. It was all too much. His control decimated, pleasure exploded inside him as his climax hit and he saw stars.

"Jenna," he roared as his semen filled her ass. He proceeded to pump until every drop had been expelled from his shaft.

He leaned over her, still embedded, and gripped her head. He turned her face toward his and slanted his mouth over hers. In that simple touch, Carter knew she hadn't been the only one who'd been claimed, for she had laid siege and wrapped herself around his being.

Then he was undoing her restraints and helping her off the horse. He helped her dress when her legs wobbled like a new born foal's. It gave him a sense of deep-seated male pride to see that he affected her so deeply.

They climbed back into the cart, but Carter wanted her seated with him for the rest of their drive. He pulled her onto his lap. She snuggled against his chest and he couldn't get past how right she felt in his arms.

By the time they'd completed their tour and parked beneath his villa, Jenna was fast asleep against him. Her soft snores and warm puffs of breath against his chest did something to him. Her trust hit him right in the chest.

He lightly caressed her cheek. She had wriggled her way inside him. He wondered if he could convince her to see him after his stay on the island. Heaven help him, he wanted to see her on his ranch. Have her there waiting on the porch as he finished up his day, and sit on the swing with her to watch the fading light as the sun set behind the Tetons. He wasn't sure what that meant, only that he wanted to see her in his world.

Could he persuade her to see him beyond his time on the island?

Chapter 8

The following day, Jenna drove her cart to Carter's after a late night shift at the Dungeon Club serving drinks. She was beat. Her body ached, her feet throbbed. Then there was the rest of her. And not all of her aches were from work, but the marathon sexcapades with Carter.

Her sasquatch was leaving. Soon. A whole lot sooner than she wanted to think about—much less consider how she felt about it all; about him and the relationship they found themselves in.

Carter's entry into her life had blindsided her. He was unexpected. A balm for her battered soul and, if she were fanciful, she'd say he was her reward for all the hardships she'd survived.

Jenna admitted, to herself at least, she had feelings for Carter. Deep ones too. She didn't want to care about the big lug. Yet she did, more than she was willing to admit. He was stern and as steady as they came. Like her own personal rock of Gibraltar, he made her yearn for things better left undisturbed. And she yearned for his touch, which was insane. They'd been going at each other like rabbits. Every single time, she was amazed that she could want him again, craved to feel more of him.

Mainly because there was no point. Her course was set,

thanks to her father's staggeringly high medical bills as he descended more into dementia each day. She paid for him to live in an assisted living facility with round the clock care. Dale Mallory had no longer known who his daughters were for a good two years now, give or take.

The money he had saved up for his retirement and to pay for her sister's tuition had dried up long ago. It was Jenna who made sure he had everything he needed for his care. And even though she wasn't there to visit him, her sister had stayed in town and gone to a local college to earn her bachelor's degree.

Once her sister graduated, they planned to sell their parents' home. The one Jenna was currently making mortgage payments on so her sister could live there while going to school, along with paying for Meghan's tuition and their father's care. Even working here on the island there never seemed to be enough money. No matter how hard she worked, there always seemed to be another bill she needed to take care of.

And Meghan helped with the bills by waiting tables. But for a college student going to school full time, the ability to pay your way was nigh on impossible. Besides, Jenna had made her dad a promise when he'd received his diagnosis and they talked about what was going to happen next. She'd sworn that she would make sure Meghan graduated and that she would use his retirement funds for Meghan's schooling.

Unfortunately, her dad had been a high school history teacher who'd never made much money. From the time Jenna had been sixteen she'd helped him pick up the slack. She'd gone to college part-time as she'd worked to help take the burden off her dad. Both were determined to make sure Meghan was okay. But then his diagnosis had come six years ago and the burden of everything had fallen on Jenna. She'd left college with only forty credits left to take to get her accounting degree and had ensured that Meghan graduated high school and applied to college. Jenna had also made the decision—when her dad's care had become too much for her to be able to handle him and support them all at the same time—to put him in the assisted living facility.

And she knew Carter was curious about her, about why she worked as much as she did. But she didn't want to burden him with her problems. There wasn't anything that could be done about them anyhow. Her dad was declining, more rapidly than she was prepared to deal with. She doubted, judging by the doctor's prognosis, that he had more than a year left.

Maybe once he was gone and her sister had graduated, she could rest a little bit. Not have to work so hard. Guilt swamped her at the thought. She shouldn't think that way—but she was just so tired.

When she entered the villa, she didn't see Carter and went searching for him. He wasn't in the lodge, but the lights were on. She went out on the back deck. And there he was: six and a half feet of naked cowboy lounging in the hot tub. His mammoth arms were spread out wide over the top of the ledge. His handsome face was cast in shadows with the light from the kitchen window spilling over the deck.

"I was wondering what time you'd be back tonight." His rough voice shivered through her.

"Sorry, it was extra busy, and Jared had to finally step in to get the place closed down for the night."

"Why don't you come join me?" he said. But didn't make a move toward her.

Jenna wanted nothing more. This man, her sasquatch, drew her like a bear to honey. She'd gladly brave a swarm of bees just to feel his touch. She stepped out of her heels. Then walked slowly toward him, discarding first her top, then her short shorts. Her bra and panties went next. And then his cuffs, because the water would ruin the buttery soft leather and she had become quite fond of wearing them. Her wrists felt naked without them.

When she reached the hot tub, Carter still had barely moved a muscle. His gaze was unreadable in the shadowy light. Jenna descended the three steps into the hot bubbling water. But she didn't stop her forward progression until she stood before him, waist deep in the frothy foam. Carter didn't move. The man didn't so much as twitch as he waited to see what she would do.

His massive frame drew her. Made her body burn with a hunger brighter than the sun. She didn't understand her need for him. How he'd come to dominate her in every way in such a short span of time, she wasn't certain. All she knew was that nothing short of a dinosaur-killing-sized asteroid could tear her away from him.

Jenna straddled his hips and had to bite back her moan at the feel of his erection between her thighs. He was so big. It was always a startling thrill. And at the intimate touch, her body turned molten.

Carter was still motionless. She leaned against his broad chest. His firmness met her softness as her breasts smooshed against him. Her hands slid around his neck. Her gaze on his, she searched his face as she closed the distance until she felt the warm puff of his breath. She closed her eyes at the last possible second as she brushed her mouth over his. He still hadn't shaved and his stubble abraded her flesh, causing tingles to erupt and sending pleasure cascading directly to her core.

Jenna traced his lips with her tongue and nibbled his fuller bottom lip before seeking entrance to his mouth. Then, finally, his arms enveloped her, crushing her body to him. One big hand cupped her nape as he took control. His tongue thrust inside. And the rest of the world—the humming of night insects, the effervescent scent of the jungle surrounding them—all ceased to exist.

Jenna kissed him with her entire being. Dueling with him. Moaning into his dominant embrace as he took their kiss deeper. She no longer knew where she ended and he began. And it didn't matter. With every carnal, wicked thrust of his tongue inside her, she ceded him another piece of her soul.

His mouth left hers and scorched a trail of open-mouthed, hungry kisses over her neck. He tugged her head back with his large fist, exposing the full column of her neck. His stubble scraped against her, causing a waterfall of pleasure to zing along her spine into her core. She rubbed her pelvis against him, his erection sliding through her folds, and she moaned at the wicked sensation.

"Please, Sir." She gasped her desire for him beyond anything quantifiable.

"Tell me," he ordered as he bit her earlobe.

"Fuck me. Please Carter, Sir, I need you," she begged.

"Lift up your hips for me," he demanded.

Without hesitation she did as he commanded and was rewarded when he fit the head of his erection at her opening.

"Look at me." His voice was low and infused with desire.

Jenna lifted her eyelids and stared at his handsome face. With her gaze trained on him, he guided her down his length until she was seated on him, his big cock fully embedded inside her sheath. She mewled at the pleasure-pain spiking her system. Her own lubrication, mixed with the water of the hot tub, made it that way. Her gaze never left his as he started to move, thrusting his shaft in long strokes meant to drive her out of her ever-loving mind.

She canted her hips, meeting him thrust for thrust, pleasured mewls escaping her mouth. Carter's hands slid to her butt. He palmed her ass, driving his cock in brutal thrusts that left her head spinning.

Steam rose around them from the hot tub. Jenna's hands slid into his hair and she brought his mouth down to hers, needing to feel all of him, to make it be enough—when she sincerely doubted just a week with him ever would be enough.

She poured herself into her kiss. He hungrily ate at her mouth, thrusting his tongue inside in time with his cock pounding inside her sheath. She writhed against him, meeting his deep strokes, canting her hips, and riding him with a fury that stole the very air from her lungs.

She no longer needed oxygen unless it came from his lips. She no longer wanted anything but the man surrounding her, loving her, and commandeering every part of her being. He drank her cries of pleasure with his mouth—his spectacular mouth that knew just how to move against her, how to draw every ounce of pleasure from her body.

Her climax hit, and it was akin to tectonic plates moving. Her pussy spasmed around his cock and she wailed against his lips. Carter's grip on her ass tightened, his cock plunged to the hilt, and streams of hot cum jettisoned into her channel, causing a secondary round of spasms.

Carter broke their kiss and bellowed as he came, then buried his face in the crook of her neck. His arms held her tight.

She knew, as she held him back, her head against his shoulder, that she had ceded him more than merely her submission. She wished that they could stay this way, freeze-frame time so that the inevitable forthcoming separation would never occur. That right now, here with him, she'd never been happier.

She had two choices. She could bemoan their tragic fate, or she could enjoy what little time they had left together. Carter shifted and looked at her then, cupping her cheek with his large palm, and Jenna chose door number two.

How could she not? That man looked at her with his lusty gaze and she turned to mush.

Her stomach chose that moment to growl. Loudly.

"When was the last time you had anything to eat?" he murmured.

She shrugged a shoulder. "There wasn't time before my shift because we were rather preoccupied."

"Allow me to rectify the matter. I can't have my sub wither away from lack of sustenance."

"No, we wouldn't want that," she agreed.

"No, we wouldn't. Especially since I plan to spend the rest of the night loving you," he said, his voice low and husky with desire.

"Good plan." It was a great plan. One she was fully on board with.

He assisted her out of the hot tub and then towed her inside, where he fulfilled every promise. Every. Single. One.

Chapter 9

When Jenna wasn't with him, Carter explored the island. There were innovations Jared had used which Carter found rather remarkable. He was already making plans to contact Tyler and have him come to his ranch for a few days. There were ideas he'd had for a while about making his land more sustainable, and now he knew Tyler was the man for the job.

He and Jenna got into a pattern. When she wasn't at work, they met back at his villa for the hottest fucking sex on the planet, as far as he was concerned. Carter couldn't remember ever feeling so relaxed.

He'd revised his initial view of the island and this unanticipated trip. As far as he was concerned, it was the best vacation he'd ever spent. He'd walked barefoot in the sand. Made love to Jenna in the surf.

She was wild and untamable, even as she surrendered, giving him everything. And he fell further under her spell. He wanted more than just this week. The fact that he had to leave tomorrow was not lost on him.

He liked waking, as he did now, to feel her killer body

wrapped around his, replicating Saran Wrap. The way the silk of her hair clung to his chest. Her scent invading the darkest recesses of his heart.

Every time he planned to ask her to come stay with him on his ranch, the words got caught in his throat. Carter had always been confident in everything that he did. But Jenna exposed his vulnerability in a way no other submissive ever had. He felt raw and uncertain. As much as she had given him in the last week, neither of them had put their feelings into words.

He wasn't exactly sure what he felt. All he knew was that he wanted—nay, needed—more time with her. The weight of it hung heavy in his chest.

She stirred in his arms. Just a slight movement, but one he'd become familiar with and which he thought was utterly charming. Jenna was not a morning person. She was doing her impersonation of an ostrich and attempting to burrow her face between his chest and arm to delay the inevitable.

"I know you're awake, darlin'. There's no point in denying it. And besides, if you wake now, it should give me just enough time."

"Time for what?" she said, muffled against his chest.

"For a few orgasms."

Her nails curled into his chest and her body melted against his. "Oh well, I guess I can wake up for that."

He chuckled as he rolled their bodies and repositioned them so that she was underneath him. Her gaze was sleep-ridden but infused with need. She was so beautiful she took his breath away. Dipping his head, he covered her mouth with his lips. He wanted her in a way he didn't fully understand, but in all his thirty-four years there had never been another woman to turn his head in this fashion. He poured his need for her, his desire for more, his yearning to stake his claim on her body and soul into his kiss.

Jenna returned his embrace with such mind-blowing ardor, he found himself trembling against her. There was no denying their chemistry was off the charts. He wanted to maintain control and dominate her but she was flaying him alive with her moans, with the way her hands gripped his back and her nails dug in. She'd wrapped her legs around his waist and that fit his cock directly against her wet folds.

Growling into her mouth he shifted his hips and thrust inside. Her pussy clasped his cock, drawing him deeper, and he knew deep down it had never been like this with anyone else. And then he rolled his hips, pumping his shaft in her welcoming heat. The little moans she made against his lips spurred him on.

But he wanted to watch her face. He lifted his mouth from hers. Drawing her arms down from around his shoulders, he threaded their fingers together and held them close to her shoulders. Her breath became his as he shuttled his shaft and she met him thrust for thrust. Passion glazed her face. Her eyes were vibrant, the blue magnetic, sucking him in until all he could see was her.

Her hands gripped his, and he felt her breathy moans all the way to his core. Her tremors started and she stiffened.

"Carter," she moaned. Her eyes went wide. Her pussy clamped and spasmed around his cock.

Her climax sent him over the edge. "Jenna," he groaned as he came. Hard. His semen poured in streaming jets inside her spasming pussy.

Before he'd even had a chance to recover, his cell phone blared on the night stand. It was unusual for him to get calls of any kind. Still cradled between Jenna's sweet thighs, he answered, staring down at her lovely face.

"Hello."

"Carter. It's Jared. Sorry to bother you but we have a slight situation. There's a hurricane bearing down on the island and we are evacuating all the guests and staff. I have one of our jets standing by at the airstrip to fly you back to the mainland. It leaves in an hour. I will send one of the bellhops to your villa to get you there."

"Okay. Anything I can do to help?" Carter asked.

"No. If Jenna's with you, she needs to get to the dock and board one of the ferries on the double. First one is leaving in fifteen minutes."

"It's that serious then?"

"Yes. And I need all my people off the island and in shelters on Nassau by noon."

"I will make sure she gets there," he replied.

"Good deal. I'm sorry that your week is being cut short by a day," Jared said.

"It's out of your control, man. Look, you have a great place here that I will recommend to my club. I'm sure you will be inundated. And I appreciate you bringing me down here. It was a trip I sorely needed," he said. His last statement was true in more ways than one.

"Glad you enjoyed it. You're welcome back anytime. Safe travels," Jared replied.

"You too. I hope it all works out," Carter said and hung up. His gaze had never left Jenna's while he'd talked to Jared. This was it.

"What's going on?" she asked.

"The island's being evacuated. There's a hurricane heading this way."

"Oh my god. We need to get a move on. If Jared is evacuating the island, it's bad," she said. "You need to pack. I can help."

"You're supposed to go meet the ferry at the docks, Jenna," Carter said, his heart aching.

"I know the protocol. I have time. Let's get going." She all but shoved him off her and he let her. The connection, the bubble they'd been in this week, had burst at the unforeseen intrusion that Mother Nature was presenting.

Carter rolled off the bed and sprang into action, the words he needed to say still lodged in his throat.

JENNA DRESSED IN A HURRY, wishing she had more time to tell Carter how she felt. But Mother Nature had thrown a wrench into everything. Maybe she could go with him to Wyoming. If he asked, she wanted to say yes with everything that she was.

Her phone rang while Carter was in the shower. It was her dad's nursing home. Every time she saw the number pop up on her screen, her heart dropped into her toes, wondering if this was it, the final separation.

"Hello?" she said, her heart in her throat.

"Ms. Mallory, this is Diane Sherman with Happy Days Assisted Living."

"Yes, what can I do for you, Diane? Is my father okay, is he —" *Dead?* She swallowed.

"Dale is just fine. I'm calling about this month's bill. We haven't received it yet…"

"I know, I'm waiting until I get paid next week. I hope that's okay. I just had my sister's tuition payment this past week," she explained, feeling her hopes sink into the bottomless pit that was her reality. Jenna wasn't leaving. She wasn't going anywhere. Her life was one big ball of fuckery, and not the good kind.

"That's fine. Will you be doing it via electronic transfer?" Diane asked.

"Yes. As soon as it's in my account, I swear. I've never been late on it," Jenna said, feeling like she had the weight of a two-ton gorilla on her back.

"I know, Ms. Mallory. That's why I called. That's fine. There will be a late fee assessed. I can't waive that, unfortunately," the woman explained.

Jenna squeezed her eyes shut to stop the tears. No point in

crying over what she couldn't control. She replied, defeated in more ways than one, "It's fine. You'll have it then."

"Fantastic. Please call me if there are any changes," Diane said cheerfully. It made Jenna want to vomit.

"I will. Thank you," Jenna said and hung up, sliding the phone into her back pocket.

Carter strode back into the room and shoved his toiletry bag in his suitcase. He was so gorgeous in his jeans and black fitted tee shirt and signature boots. She had to blink back the moisture from her gaze.

"Problem?" he asked.

"No. It's nothing," she covered and gave him a smile. She didn't want him to remember her as being sad. Or that she was a woman whose life wasn't her own. She wanted him to think of her fondly and perhaps with a smile over the surprising week they'd shared together.

He strode over to her with his sexy swagger. When he was a foot away from her, she handed him his cuffs. Her wrists felt barren and naked without them. She said, "You'll be needing these back."

"Come with me," he demanded, closing his hands around hers, his cuffs squashed between them.

"Where?" she asked. But deep down, she knew, and she prayed for strength to do what was right by her family.

"To my ranch. Leave on the plane with me. Come spend time with me in Wyoming and we can see—"

"I can't, Carter. I'm sorry," she replied. Her heart ached with the weight of her responsibilities. His words that he wanted more were like an arrow piercing her chest. It should have made her happy, ecstatic even. Instead it left her feeling broken inside.

"Can't or won't?" he asked, his face still but his eyes blazing with fury.

"Does it really matter when the outcome is the same? I wish things were different, but they aren't, and my world is here. I'm sorry. I know it's not what you want to hear." She clamped her lips shut and glanced down, hiding the moisture flooding her gaze. She blinked back her tears.

His arms slid around her, and she had to fight back the sob lodged in her throat. Then he tipped her face up to his and his eyes searched hers. And what did he see? That she loved him, and didn't know how to say the words because it wouldn't change the outcome and would only hurt them both? That she'd never met anyone like him and if things were different, if her stupid life were different, she could see herself building a life with him? But Jenna had learned long ago that wishes and dreams only crushed a person when there was no hope of anything more.

"We have something here, Jenna. I don't understand why you want to throw it away," Carter said. His knuckles traced her cheek and it rocked her to her foundation.

She didn't want to throw it away, but her choices and her life were not her own. Before she allowed the tears threatening to spill over, she leaned up on her tiptoes and kissed him, pouring every ounce of her heart into the embrace. She kissed him for all the tomorrows they wouldn't have, and with all the love she felt for him.

She kissed him knowing it was the last time. That when he left and walked out that door, he was taking a piece of her soul with him. She kissed him hoping to imprint a part of herself upon him. That he would remember this time—and her—with fondness.

Carter kissed her back with such dominant possession that when they broke apart at the knock on the door, it took every-thing inside Jenna not to throw herself at his feet and say she had changed her mind, to beg him to take her with him.

"Mister Jones, I'll get your luggage for you if you're ready. The jet is prepared to leave as soon as we get you to the airstrip," Sean Davos said, interrupting their goodbye.

"I'll be right out, if you want to take those." Carter indicated his suitcase and carry-on bag.

"Certainly, sir," Sean said and hefted Carter's luggage into the elevator.

When they were alone once more, Carter's gaze shifted back to Jenna's and he said, "Are you sure I can't change your mind?"

She had to fight back the urge to renege on her previous stance, fling her arms around his torso and beg him to take her with him. Every instinct insisted she leave with him. Yet she denied herself. She curled her fingers into her palms, digging her nails into her flesh. She used that sharp pain to focus and to keep herself from touching him again. Otherwise, she wouldn't have the strength to let him go.

And it was for the best. He had a life and so did she, one where she was needed and counted on.

"I'm sure. I enjoyed our week together, Carter," she said.

"Jenna, I... wish things were different." His face was solemn as he stared at her.

"Be happy, Carter. You better go, you don't want to miss your flight," she said, feeling the tethers on her emotions begin to slip.

"Take care, Jenna," he murmured and then turned away from her. Arrows pierced her chest. He strode, as sure-footed as ever, to the kitchen table, picked up his black Stetson and set it on his head.

At the elevator, he turned back to her, giving her one last look. She smiled, fighting back the moisture filling her gaze, needing to soak up every moment. And he seemed to be doing the same. The very air stilled at the wealth of emotion in that one look. Then he tipped his hat and entered the lift. The doors slid shut behind his massive form.

And Jenna wondered if it was possible to die of a broken heart. She stumbled to her knees and bowed her head as the tears started. She stayed there, on the floor, sobbing her heart out until she was wrung out. She couldn't care less if a hurricane was bearing down on the island. She felt crippled. She only knew she was still alive because of the pain slicing her to ribbons. The only reason she stopped crying at all was because all the moisture in her body had likely been expelled through her tears.

As she picked herself up off the floor, her bones ached down to the very marrow. Jenna went into the bathroom to wash her face. On her way, she spied something black sticking out from beneath the bed. She changed course and knelt down near the bedpost. On all fours, she reached underneath. Her fingers brushed the cotton material and she withdrew it.

Carter's scent hit her first. It was his, without a doubt. She pressed it into her face and inhaled him. He'd unknowingly left her something to remember him by. She lowered the shirt, still gripping it to her chest. She'd keep it. Forever.

Jenna washed her face in the bathroom sink and then departed his villa. She'd not be able to return to this one. Not for a long time without the memories suffocating her. She headed back to her apartment, packed a bag to take with her, and shoved Carter's shirt in with the rest of her things.

Then she drove back across the island, taking a different route than usual and subtly ignoring the places they'd gone. If she wasn't careful, the memories of their time together would swallow her whole.

When she arrived at the hotel, Jared was there, directing the frenzy.

"Jenna, lass, why haven't you departed on one of the ferries? Get yourself down to the docks at once."

"Yes, Sir. Sorry."

"Are you all right, lass?" Jared asked.

"Why wouldn't I be?" she asked, bluffing. See Jenna bluff and pretend her heart wasn't bleeding out.

"No reason," Jared murmured, his gaze intent. "Get to the boats."

Jenna did as he asked, not putting up a fuss or playing any pranks. She just didn't have the heart for frivolity.

That was because her heart was airborne and headed to Wyoming. When she boarded the ferry and watched the island diminish as they sped away, she wondered for the hundredth time if she'd made the right choice.

Then she received a text message.

Meghan: the registrar received the payment for my schooling. Thanks, sis! Xoxo

Jenna replied: *Good. Now get back to studying, or else…*

Meghan: Yes, ma'am.

Jenna turned her gaze toward the bow; looking forward, not back. The decision she'd made was the right one, the only one she could make under the circumstances. And if her heart squeezed and ached at the thought of Carter, well, there was nothing for it. It was her new normal.

Because she knew deep down that he was it for her. That this week, she'd unwittingly given him her whole heart. And now she would love him for the rest of her days.

No regrets—save one. She'd never told him she loved him. But she liked to think that, perhaps on some level, he knew. It didn't matter, really, the love was there regardless. And she would cherish the week she'd had, the week she'd loved, and pull it out to remember whenever the weight of her responsibilities grew to be too much.

One day, the thought of him wouldn't slice her to the bone. One day.

Chapter 10

C arter returned to his ranch and all but buried himself in his work. He didn't go to the club. Didn't see anyone. He threw himself into working his ranch as if he were possessed.

And perhaps on some level he was, with memories of Jenna dogging his every step, his every waking hour, and even his dreams. They were eating him alive. Even when he thought he had expelled her from his waking life, she visited him as he slept. He reached for her in the dead of night, wishing he still had her there beside him.

Two months passed before he finally admitted to himself that there was no getting over her. One night, in the middle of the night, he sent Jared an email, asking him for a contact number for her.

Jared replied to his request the following day.

Carter,

Good to hear from you. Unfortunately, Jenna left the island last week and is no longer working here. It was her decision to leave, by the way, I didn't fire her. She didn't leave me with a forwarding address, but I do have a phone number for you.

Be kind to her. She's going through something that even I am not aware of —nor have I been able to figure it out.

Best regards,

Jared McTavish

Carter stared at the screen and the phone number Jared had listed for Jenna Mallory, wondering what she was going through. Why had she left the island? She'd been super protective of her job there.

He typed the number into his phone and stared at it. His thumb hovered over the call button. And what would he say? That he missed her? That he needed her like he needed air to breathe? That he couldn't get through a day without thinking about her?

Frustrated with himself, he saved her number into his phone and got to work. Every day, he would stare at the number, paralyzed by fear and regret. Until, after a month of staring at her number each day, he realized why he couldn't let her go.

Fuck, he was a little slow on the uptake. Maybe because he hadn't felt this way in, well, ever. He loved her. The unexpected nature of his love for her was swift and sudden. Considering he was a man who didn't do love and softer emotions, she'd been like a rocket straight into his heart.

He pressed the call button, holding his breath as it rang. And then the message that this was not a working number filtered through the receiver. He sat back in his desk chair. He'd waited too long. He stared at his phone, then chucked it against the wall and watched it explode.

Carter had loved Jenna and lost her before he'd even realized it. She'd been unexpected, and he had been a fucking moron. He never should have left the island without her.

He swore to himself that he would find her. Somehow, some way, he would track her down. And then, he was never letting her go.

Anya Summers

Born in St. Louis, Missouri, Anya grew up listening to Cardinals baseball and reading anything she could get her hands on. She remembers her mother saying if only she would read the right type of books instead binging her way through the romance aisles at the bookstore, she'd have been a doctor. While Anya never did get that doctorate, she graduated cum laude from the University of Missouri-St. Louis with an M.A. in History.

Anya is a bestselling and award-winning author published in multiple fiction genres. She also writes urban fantasy and paranormal romance under the name Maggie Mae Gallagher. A total geek at her core, when she is not writing, she adores attending the latest comic con or spending time with her family. She currently lives in the Midwest with her two furry felines.

Don't miss these exciting titles by Anya Summers and Blushing Books!

The Dungeon Fantasy Club Collection
The complete set of all eight full-length, scintillating, spicy romance novels!
Her Highland Master
To Master and Defend
Two Doms for Kara
His Driven Domme
Her Country Master
Love Me, Master Me
Submit to Me

Her Wired Dom

The Pleasure Island Collection
The complete set of nine full-length novels!
Her Master and Commander, Book 1
Her Music Masters, Book 2
Their Shy Submissive, (Novella) Book 3
Her Lawful Master, Book 4
Her Rockstar Dom, Book 5
Duets and Dominance, Book 6
Her Undercover Doms (Novella) Book 7
Ménage in Paradise, Book 8
Her Rodeo Masters, Book 9

Cuffs & Spurs Series
His Scandalous Love, Book 1
His Unexpected Love, Book 2
His Wicked Love, Book 3
His Untamed Love, Book 4
His Tempting Love, Book 5
His Seductive Love, Book 6
His Secret Love, Book 7
His Cherished Love, Book 8
His Christmas Love, Holiday Novella

Crescent City Kings Series
Lone Survivor, Book 1

Alcyran Chronicles Series
Taken By The Beast, Book 1
Claimed By The Beast, Book 2
Loved By The Beast, Book 3

Audio Books

Her Highland Master

Visit her on social media here:
http://www.facebook.com/AnyaSummersAuthor
Twitter: @AnyaBSummers
Goodreads: https://www.goodreads.com/author/show/
15183606.Anya_Summers
Sign-up for Anya Summers Newsletter

Connect with Anya Summers:
www.anyasummers.com

Blushing Books

Blushing Books is one of the oldest eBook publishers on the web. We've been running websites that publish spanking and BDSM related romance and erotica since 1999, and we have been selling eBooks since 2003. We hope you'll check out our hundreds of offerings at http://www.blushingbooks.com.

CPSIA information can be obtained
at www.ICGtesting.com
Printed in the USA
BVHW031731031219
565404BV00007BA/1308/P